22

DESERT TRAILS

Having to kill his double-crossing partner almost soured Wade Tulane. He headed for Texas, and it was his destiny to tangle with Rip Heggety, a gunny who sought hidden Indian gold. It was a more pleasant fate to meet up with Stella, but not before he had to rescue her from undesirables. When Tommy and Dave Latimer became his pals, the Siomi Indian treasure became a goal they had to reach, and Wade set out on a dangerous desert trail, a wanted man . . .

Books by John Blaze
in the Linford Western Library:

COLT FLAME
LAWLESS HIDEOUT
HELL-BENT GENTS

JOHN BLAZE

DESERT TRAILS

Complete and Unabridged

LINFORD
Leicester

First published in Great Britain in 1990 by
Robert Hale Limited
London

First Linford Edition
published March 1994
by arrangement with
Robert Hale Limited
London

British Library CIP Data

Blaze, John
Desert trails.—Large print ed.—
Linford western library
I. Title II. Series
823.914 [F]

ISBN 0–7089–7497–X

Published by
F. A. Thorpe (Publishing) Ltd.
Anstey, Leicestershire

Set by Words & Graphics Ltd.
Anstey, Leicestershire
Printed and bound in Great Britain by
T. J. Press (Padstow) Ltd., Padstow, Cornwall

This book is printed on acid-free paper

1

Trail to Trouble

HE rode up out of the desert, a tall grim man stooped in the saddle, on a trail-tired horse. Rider and animal were sure *real* tired. Dust coated his Stetson and caked with the sweat on the red kerchief around his neck. His black shirt had its quota of desert dust and sweat from the ride.

Laredo! It was somewheres ahead!

At a touch of the leathers the black horse paused on the shale ridge. Wade Tulane stared across the heat hazes to the toy-like spread of buildings that marked the outskirts of Laredo. With stiff fingers, he fumbled for the makings and began to shape a brown-paper cigarette.

Laredo! It was the name of a

boom-town. Down here in Texas, close to the Mexican border, men and money swirled around the cattle business, the newly-opened railroad and the discovery of gold. The heady combination attracted the hardy and the greedy — and men like Wade Tulane.

He nudged his horse into the slow plodding gait which the animal could maintain all day if needed. The horseflesh was damned tired, sweat-flecked and smelling of hot saddle-leather.

They went down the shale slope to the sandy bed of the gully where the heat from the earth rose like an oven. Silvery cholla cactus, miraculously extracting moisture from roots deep in the sandy soil, filled rocky clefts. Away to his right, two gaunt Joshua trees stood like spiky cacti sentinels.

Wade hunched in the saddle and brooded, content to allow the passage of time to bring him into Laredo. In any case the black horse could not be hurried. Wade's dark eyes assumed a reflective gleam as he thought: "Laredo might be the place for me . . . at least it's a long way from Colorado . . . might be the place for a man to stop . . . think awhile . . . "

The cayuse moved slowly, so tired and deliberate, and then came out of the gully and plodded over the sand and shale. After half a mile they rounded a straggle of rocky outcrops lying on the desert as if thrown by a giant hand.

Wade Tulane sighted the other rider coming around the outcrop and his eyes narrowed. His lips became a tight firm line as the yards between them lessened. He had a natural poker-face, with a taut mouth that indicated his iron character.

The stranger was badly wounded, that much Wade saw in a glance. He rolled in the saddle, holding the rawhide ribbons with one hand while the other clutched a red patch on his left shoulder.

He was urging his bronc along the narrow trail between rocks when, surprised, he saw Wade. He made to force his way past Wade's horse, but a hand went out and grabbed the animal's headstall and brought the crittur to a halt.

"Let me get past!" The wounded person was young, that was clear, with the shrill voice of a boy in his late teens.

"How come you're hit?" Wade continued to hold the horse. With a sharp glance he noted the Colt in the stiff, new leather holster. "You got into a bit of trouble, young feller?"

"Let me ride on," snapped the other.

Again he tried to urge his animal forward but Wade kept the head down. The horse jibbed restlessly under this treatment.

"You'll be durned lucky if you reach town without falling off that nag," rapped Wade. "Let me help you, amigo . . ."

"Doggone it," shrilled the young

man. "Let me get away! I can look after myself! I ain't hurt so bad. It was — just — just an accident. A gun went off . . . "

Wade narrowed his eyes. He knew when someone was lying, for long experience in encountering strangers on lonesome trails had made him shrewd. And this boy did not lie well. Wade figured the youngster had got his wound in anything but an accident.

He released the headstall of the other horse. The young man jabbed spur rowels to flanks and the cayuse sprang away. Wade sat tall in the saddle for all his tiredness and watched the young guy ride away as quickly as possible for one in his injured condition.

Wade rubbed a hand over his bristly chin and ruminated. "Wal, ain't my grief. I meet all kinds. Obstinate young colt, anyways."

He rode into Laredo some time later and his first thought was for his trail-tired horse. He found a livery and led the black inside, removing the saddle, blanket and headstall, and then handed over to the wrangler with instructions to rub down, water and feed the animal.

Then Wade walked out into the dusty street and stared at the nearest hotel. Bonanza Hotel! He'd seen hotels like these wherever there was gold or the rumour of the yellow metal. The big two-storey place with the ornate façade looked just what he needed. Inside he would find rest, food and drink. Yeah — drink — for Wade Tulane was no saint and lived hard at times.

He walked stiffly into the hotel, carrying his saddle-gear and a small canvas poke which contained his few possessions, such as a change of shirt and socks.

He pushed through the batwing doors; stared around the sparsely patronised bar-room and then approached a small desk which was there for the convenience of visitors who wanted more than just a slug of whisky. There was no one at the desk. Wade waited a few seconds and then thumped tiredly on the polished pine.

A thickset man, looking hot in a black suit and a black silk necktie, came up to the wanderer.

"Anythin' I can do for you, stranger?" The man seemed truculent. Wade stared.

"Yeah. I want a room and hot water brought up and somewhere to dump this gear . . . "

"You can do that in your room," snapped the other. "We ain't got skivvies here."

"No politeness either, huh?" Wade and the other man glared long at each other as if animosity was the order of the day. Then the man backed down. "Follow me, Mister . . . "

"Wade Tulane." The trail-weary man searched the other's face. There was no reason why the name should mean anything to an hotel-keeper in Laredo but one never knew. News travelled strangely and maybe there was a

Colorado man in this corner of Texas. But the name meant nothing apparently to the surly hotel-keeper.

"I'll show you a room, Mister Tulane. You sure need a wash-up. You've been riding a long time, I guess. Law ain't after you, is it? You look the type . . . "

Wade grinned thinly. "My hoglegs, huh?"

"Keep them in the leather, mister. I don't like gunplay in this hotel. We get some class of customers in here — rangers, bankers, cattlemen . . . "

"But not gunslingers," Wade grimaced, deciding he didn't like this specimen of Laredo. "All right — let's go. I'm blamed tired and I hanker for that wash-up . . . "

They walked up creaking stairs to a wide landing and from there the wandering man was shown a room — one bed, one chest of drawers and not much else. Ten minutes later, to give the hotel-keeper his due, a two-gallon jug of steaming water was brought up by a whiskered old-timer in a faded shirt and grubby cords. The oldster shuffled into the room, the odour of tobacco on him, and set the big jug down on the wash-stand and then turned to Wade. It was a signal for both men to give way to astonished cries.

"Ezra Sloan — you old galoot!"

"Migosh — Wade Tulane himself!"

Wade's smile faded as fast as it had arrived. Wary, he looked at the old man. "You been working here long, Ezra?"

"Just about two months," grinned the oldster.

"You got tired of Cactus Plain up there in Colorado?"

"I allus was a wanderer," declared the other. "I jest figured I'd been around Cactus Plain too long. How come you're down thisaway? Last time I saw you it was at a placer claim an' you had a partner. You sure seemed to be doing all right. Remember that night in the camp saloon? That big tent with the card-games and likker and fancy women? You lost a stash of money an' didn't seem to care none. I remember you said plenty gold-dust in the river. What happened brought you down here?"

Wade turned to the wash-stand. "It began to peter out. I got sick of Colorado and just rode out. Guess I kept on moving — and now I'm down here . . . "

It wasn't an entirely accurate account but it would do to shut up the old-timer.

"Why in tarnation didn't your partner come down with you, Wade?"

The young man turned a grim face to the other. "Jack Rawkin is dead, got himself killed."

"A Colt slug?"

"Yeah . . . " Wade tightened his lips. He hoped he wouldn't have to tell many more lies.

"Wal, as I remember, Jack Rawkin was a healthy galoot. But a Colt slug is sure bad medicine to any man."

"It certainly is . . . " Wade paused, forgetting about the grey-haired oldster as his mind filled with recollections of the days at the placer claim. The river had been a busy place then, with men panning for gold for nearly three miles up that rocky yellowish river. Every quarter-mile there were men, standing in the shallow pools, the wide handle-less pans working all day in search of the elusive yellow dust and occasional nuggets.

Jack Rawkin and he had gotten on all right — at the start! They'd worked and joked, rested and swopped yarns, drunk raw whisky in the saloon tent and slowly collected a few small pokes filled with yellow dust and nuggets. They'd been good partners until . . . Wade tightened his lips at the memories . . .

He'd left Jack Rawkin to get some supply of grub. The man had been working with the pan, swilling yellow water, sand and dust. Wade waved. "Won't be long. Got to get some eats, huh?"

"Git some lean bacon, podner — an' to hell with the price," Jack had yelled. A big man, he bawled out everything he wanted to say. Wade left him, trudging through the rocky valley, a gun at his hip, a canvas poke held in one hand. Men stared at him; some shouted a greeting while others were surly. The surly men were the ones who were having little luck with their claims. Not every galoot along that ravine and river-bed was in luck. Some pools gave not a gleam of gold-dust. Others were rich — and there were rivalries and hatreds among the miners as a result.

Men hid their pokes in holes in the ground. Some men put it around that they got no gold out of the river — but strangely they were always working — except when they were knocking back whisky in the saloon tent. Every man had a partner, one to stand guard over their tent and other belongings — and the pokes filled with gold-dust. There wasn't much trust.

So when Wade returned from the

supply tent with bacon and beans he was surprised to discover that Jack Rawkin had gone.

Naturally, he first noticed that the guy's horse wasn't there, tethered with a feed-bag because there was precious little grass in this rocky-strewn river course, and the next thing was he saw that Jack Rawkin's saddle-bags were not in the tent. His rifle had gone, too.

And the four small bags of dust and little nuggets!

Wade Tulane stamped out of the tent and stared along the river valley. Strangely, the sound of running water seemed prominent in his ears — and then some fool of a miner singing an Irish song — and then a horse pawed on rock with a hoof. Wade cursed, not willing to believe Jack Rawkin had run out on him. Then slow anger crept into his heart. "Gold — curse it! The things a man will do for gold! I wouldn't have believed it! Not Jack!"

But the evidence was there. In the hour that Wade had been at the provision tent, the fool had taken off His gear was gone; his horse and guns had gone.

The lust for gold had gotten into the man.

Others had killed for the yellow metal. Maybe he was lucky Jack Rawkin hadn't handed him a Colt slug — or knifed him!

It wasn't something he was going to take. Slowly, he saddled his horse, shoved the rifle into the saddle-holster, got a grub-stake and a water-bottle filled. He looked again at the hole in the ground where the gold-filled pokes had been concealed and he shook his head. "Damn you, Jack Rawkin. I trusted you. You ain't going to get away with it — even if have to kill you!"

Wade rode out, leaving the tent and few possessions. He took to a rough trail above the main bed of the river. He came to a rough shack of wood and tarpaulin and hailed the man sitting there. The oldish galoot had been pally in the past.

"You seen my partner this day, mister?"

The man spat. "Him? Aw, yeah — he went past with his hoss. Seemed in a hurry . . . "

"Yeah — he would be. So long, mister . . . "

Wade could not hurry his horse over the rock-strewn ground and obviously Jack Rawkin was governed by the same conditions. But a mile or so on, when he had urged his mount out of the river valley, he got on to some grassland. He figured Jack Rawkin was bound for Cactus Plain. The assayer's office was located there. Maybe the man wanted to exchange the gold for money — but just maybe. There wasn't any distinct track to follow; many others on horseback had passed this way.

It wasn't the gold he was after. He simply wanted to challenge the man he had trusted. Trust was important.

A man who broke it was dirt. He figured to let Jack Rawkin know just what he thought of him. It seemed a mighty urgent idea . . .

Wade stood in the hotel room, his mind filled with the recollections . . . Ezra Sloan watched him . . . puzzled . . .

He remembered the curses he'd heaped upon his partner as the horse got into a slow canter, covering a few miles at a good lick as they shortened the distance to the strangely-named town Cactus Plain. There wasn't much cacti around that part of the terrain — just one stretch where by a fluke of nature the plants had taken root.

He wondered what the hell he was going to say to Jack Rawkin — or do with him supposing he caught up with the rannigan. Damned gold! Yeah — the lust for gold was like a poison. He'd figured Jack Rawkin for a good guy . . .

With bitterness settling in his heart,

he cursed the man and cursed the gold.

It was only a hunch that the robbing swine had headed for the town. There was nothing else to use as a guide.

But then there was nowhere else to go for about thirty miles around. It had to be the ugly shanty town, with the saloons, the assayer's office and somewhere to hide . . .

Late in the day, with the sun setting like a red orb over the hills surrounding Cactus Plain, Wade Tulane slowly got into the town. As always, his first thought on this vengeful trip had been for his horse. He came out of the livery later and headed slowly and thoughtfully for the nearest saloon. As it happened, he knew this was the drinking-den that he and Jack Rawkin had favoured on their few convivial visits to the town.

But his so-called partner was not in the gaudy saloon, with its sawdust-strewn wooden floor. Wade took a slug of whisky and got out. He went to the assayer's office which had the big sign: Gold bought. Claims registered. Fair deals.

"You seen a big guy with a loud voice in here maybes a few hours ago?" He watched the assayer, a clerk-like man with a pale face and little black moustache.

"We get plenty like that. Has this man got a name?"

"Yeah — Jack Rawkin."

The assayer consulted a huge leather-bound ledger where inked entries were recorded. "Sure. We bought ten ounces of gold-dust from him — paid a fair price, if you've got any complaints. But what is it to you?"

"Just wanted to know. Good-day to you . . . " And Wade went out of the wood building in a grim mood.

The whole thing was beginning to rile him, stir up a hatred in his brain, something he never thought he could direct at Jack Rawkin. It was treachery. The man had tricked him. He'd thrown away the spirit of partnership as if it had been an empty can of beans. Wade hated being tricked.

He was beginning to hate Jack Rawkin.

"Cheating swine!" he muttered. "Ten ounces of dust, huh! He'll be lousy with money . . . reckon he'll be in some saloon . . . Sure liked the booze, that man."

Wade headed for another rough saloon which had a false front and a sign: LAST CHANCE. Grimly, he thought that maybe it might prove to be correct.

It was a honky-tonk place where a so-called lady in a smelly satin dress was thumping at a piano. Only a few customers were in the place at that early time of the evening but enough to liven up the atmosphere. It figured. Jack Rawkin of the loud voice also liked loud noises.

Wade spotted him at the bar. He was flushed of face. He was evidently feeling good on the rot-gut in his belly.

Wade just waited at the bar, staring, and then the other man noticed him. Jack Rawkin seemed to sober up in seconds. Wade watched him with a fixed smile that held little mirth. The piano thumped away, some old Civil War tune that had little relevance. Men at a table dealt cards. Others boasted with their pals. Wade outstared Jack Rawkin. Then: "You figure on some trouble, Wade?" Jack Rawkin yelled the challenge across the saloon.

"You have tricked me . . . "

"Jest gold-dust," jeered Jack Rawkin loudly.

"We worked hard for that dust . . . "

"Yeah — both of us."

"A man who robs his partner is a low-down bastard." Wade's words were heard right down the bar and men turned and then shuffled away with quick glances at each other.

"You calling me names?"

"Yeah — skunk would be one!" Wade hesitated grimly. He wanted to give the other man a chance, a moment of weakness it might seem. His single gun lay snugly at his side, easy in the holster. Other times he packed twin Colts. Jack Rawkin was armed, he noted, and he knew he was pretty good with a gun — better with a rifle.

A sudden flush of animosity seemed to sweep into Jack Rawkin and his face twisted. "Damn you, Tulane. I guess I just got sick of you! I got to hate you! Surprised, huh? So I took the gold!"

"You took more than your share . . . "

"I could ha' got my share any time!"

"Damned greed!" snarled Wade, anger rising like a grim bile in his gut. "Ten ounces of dust, huh? You must still have some stashed away. We had a damn sight more than that."

"I'll be rich!"

"You might be dead, cheater!"

The man behind the bar got out an old shotgun, laid it on the pine counter and shuffled uneasily. Wade saw his play out of the corner of an eye. The other corner was fixed on Jack Rawkin.

Strangely, Wade did not know much about the other rannigan's gunfighting prowess. Their partnership had never got into that kind of situation. They had never gone gunning for anyone together. And they'd never squared up to each other — until right now!

The barman was nervous. He was acting. Wade figured he would never pick up the shotgun. It was a play designed to impress. It sure did not impress Wade Tulane . . .

Wade did not want this crazy situation because it was a road to hell. It was back down or die. Or maybe try to digest a slug in the gut . . .

The seconds in which the two men glared at each other seemed like an eternity, and right to the last second Wade hoped the other fool might back down. But he didn't.

Wade saw the nervous impulse with which Jack Rawkin's hand slid to his gun-butt, a move that needed only grim split seconds but which could not be stopped. Rawkin's Colt jerked magically into view, finger on the trigger. Wade's gun matched the other's movement, hesitation grimly vanishing. Wade's gun spoke first, the slug spitting from the barrel in smoke and flame and noise. Rawkin seemed to jerk physically, a fraction of time behind Wade, and his weapon was angled stupidly at the thin air when his slug spat out. The acrid smell of gunsmoke filled the saloon as one man staggered back under the impact of the slug from the .45 — and that man was not Wade Tulane!

Wade cursed the whole damned business as he stared down at the prone, bleeding body, and then he slowly put his Colt back in leather and looked grimly around the saloon. Some men seemed frozen at tables. The lady piano-player had fingers still on the keys — but not a chord vibrated out. The barman had not touched his shotgun. Everything seemed frozen in time.

And then a man snarled: "Damned

murder! He walks in here an' plugs this other feller!"

"Yep. That's the way I saw it," snapped another man.

Wade turned to the barman. "You know it was a fair fight . . . "

"The hell I do!" spat the man.

"He'd stolen gold-dust from me . . . "

"Yeah? That's your tale, mister . . . "

"We got a sheriff in Cactus Plain," yelled a little man in a store suit, "and we don't like gunplay. Hey — someone get the blamed sheriff! He don't like gunmen either."

Wade knew he had to get out, an instinctive feeling that events were dead against him and if he didn't travel he'd be put in a jail. Sympathy for him seemed to be nil. Sure, there was a dead man — and he regretted it more than anyone. Again cursing inwardly at the distasteful turn of events he swung towards the batwing door of the Last Chance Saloon. Once again he had this prophetic feeling that the place was accurately named — so far as he was concerned.

"Damn — damn — damn!" He mouthed the bitter words as he strode down the main street, going towards the livery. It was a bad mess he was in. Rawkin was dead — not wounded — with a too-accurate gunshot. His horse in the livery was probably still tired. He'd have to ride out on an unrested nag — and quick, before he had to deal with the sheriff.

It was a damned mess and not one he'd wanted. Maybe he should have allowed Jack Rawkin to get away with the gold and put it down to bitter experience! Maybe! That would have been a yellow-bellied way to deal with the man. And the money the cheating man had got for the stolen gold was still somewhere. But there wasn't time to forage around and find out where Rawkin had left his horse and belongings. He had to ride out!

It was a sickening end to the whole thing. He could still see the prone man on the saloon floor — his ex-partner who he'd had to kill.

Wade Tulane was not a killing man, even in a territory where sudden death due to gunfights was commonplace.

Sure, he had shot at outlaws in the past — and rustlers when he'd worked for a big spread — but never at a man who'd once been a friend.

He got his horse out of the livery, paid the wrangler and set off on a slow-moving animal into a darkening night.

He knew he'd have to make for the placer claim, pick up a few items and then move out again — quickly, before the damned sheriff came nosing around. He was just too fed up to answer questions.

He'd do that — and then ride away from Colorado, maybe trade in his horse for a better and fresher animal somewhere.

Wade Tulane's brain had raced over the whole sequence of events as he stood in the hotel — the Bonanza Hotel — right there with the puzzled Ezra Sloan watching him. His thoughts about the trailing and killing of Jack Rawkin had only occupied some fleeting moments of thought, but it had seemed a long-drawn-out dive into the past.

Ezra Sloan grinned. "You sure think a lot, Wade Tulane . . . must ha' been something on your mind. But I'm right glad to see you."

"Same here, Ezra," said Wade slowly. "But I want to forget Colorado and Cactus Plain — if you don't mind."

"Sure; if you don't want to think about it, I'll forget about it, too. Ain't so good to lose a partner . . . "

2

More Gunplay!

EZRA SLOAN seemed inclined to hang around but Wade Tulane wasn't too keen on rambling conversation. The oldster was in the way, not that he realised that fact. Wade's mind was still full of the unpleasant events up there in Colorado. He was in Laredo in order to put that all behind him.

"Say, you aim to look for gold around these parts?" asked Ezra.

"I'm right off the idea . . . "

"Wal, what do you figure to do in Laredo? You ain't the cowpunching type . . . "

"Ezra, I'd be mighty pleased if you'd mosey along and let a man wash and shave."

"Heh! Heh! Reckon I talk too much!

I'll see you again. If you want a partner, remember I know more about gold huntin' than some of these jumped-up hombres that's hellin' into town. An' if you aim to buy horses I'm a pretty good wrangler. Reckon I'm a mighty fit galoot and too young to waste my time as a hotel swamper! I aim — "

"Hell — Ezra — git! I want a wash."

The oldster gave a cackling laugh and went through the open door. Wade gave his attention to the soap and water.

This was a luxury that only a man who'd been on a weary trail could appreciate and he stripped off and began work. Water on his waist and his head seemed to wash away the bitter memories of Jack Rawkin and Colorado.

Then he shaved, using the long-handled razor he took from his canvas holdall. He was tired, but he went on with the cleaning-up job with absolute deliberation. It helped get rid of Colorado. He was still tired, in a way, using inner strength to get through the hours. Perhaps he needed a good long sleep, maybe a whole day, to put all the strain behind him, the long hours on horseback and the heat and trail-camp food. But he felt he wanted to press on also. He'd settle into some sort of routine here in Laredo, given time. Right there and then he was cleaning up. He beat the dust out of his brown trousers and climbed back into them because that was all he possessed.

He was not a range-tramp, although he had acquired the appearance of one these past few days. He got a clean shirt out of his holdall and donned it. He polished his boots with a rag and beat dust out of his Stetson. Then he buckled his cartridge-belt on to the familiar notch. It kept up his trousers! Then the gunbelt went on, the twin Colts lying fairly high on his hips because Wade Tulane was a long-bodied man and had long arms. He could reach the six-shooters just nicely. Not for him the very low-slung gun that rested almost on a man's thigh. As for the twin Colts, they looked impressive — and he could use two guns in simultaneous movement — but in truth he knew that most of the time the average range man needed only one.

Maybe the Colts would warn off trigger-happy rannigans. Or maybe they would attract some desperado who figured he was the best! Maybe it was a gamble he shouldn't be taking.

He left his room some time later and locked the door behind him. Ezra Sloan could take the used water away some other time. He locked the door because he didn't want snoopers going through his saddle-bags.

Wade Tulane went down to the bar of the Bonanza Hotel and drank a quick shot of the Laredo version of whisky rot-gut. It put some immediate energy into him. But he knew a better idea would be to take in some real grub!

Then he'd have to get some quick-paying work. He had some money on him, cash from previously disposed of gold up at Cactus Plain, but he'd have been better off if he had the gold Jack Rawkin had stolen from him. Cursing the memory, he thought he'd have to get work riding shotgun on gold shipments or guarding some rich cattleman. Anything legal . . .

He went along the boardwalk until he reached a Chinese-run eating-house. Turning into the place there was the satisfying smell of hot cooking.

He got what he needed to satisfy the inner man in the shape of jerky-beef and gravy, beans and new spuds, then apple tart. He drank from a big mug of coffee while eating. The other customers seemed to be noisy cowpokes, miners and railroad workers having time off. He didn't know any of them. He was wary of meeting anyone from the Cactus Plain area of Colorado.

Idly, he left the restaurant and stood outside, on the boardwalk, and scanned the activities of Laredo. The dusty street bore a slow-plodding mule train, six of the critturs hauling a huge wagon. A Concord stage was outside a freight office being loaded with passengers' luggage. A prospector lead a burro around a corner and stopped outside an assayer's office. Wade heard the tinkle of a piano from a saloon called La Belle, with the heat of the sun still hanging over the place. In an alley across the main stem Mexican children and some dogs played in the alkali dust.

A familiar scene in such a town where cattle and prospecting and railroad came together. At night the place would be bursting at the seams.

He was thinking of returning to the Bonanza Hotel to get some overdue shut-eye when a door in a clothing emporium across the street suddenly opened with the jangling of a doorbell and a young guy stepped out on to the plankwalk. He halted as he stared swiftly at Wade. The recognition was mutual. This was the young man he'd seen out on the desert — the young feller who'd rode past the rocky outcrops while wounded, the red tell-tale patch on his left shoulder. This was the young man who'd rolled a bit in the saddle because of his wound.

Wade knew he had a bandage under his shirt. As in the first encounter out in the desert, he tried to slip past Wade Tulane. Apparently he didn't want to be recognised.

Wade thrust out an arm. The young feller didn't wish to be detained. "Get out of my way, stranger!"

"We're not strangers exactly," drawled Wade. "Somebody shot you! You're still suffering that wound."

"Get out of my way . . . "

"Did you leave a dead man out in the desert by any chance? Somebody shot you! What happened to the other hombre? Did he get away — or what?"

"Why can't you mind your own business?"

“Yep. Maybe you’re right.” Wade lowered his arm. “Just plain curiosity, I guess. Well . . . ”

The emporium doorbell jangled again and suddenly it seemed a girl was revealed standing in the open space. Wade stared at glorious fair hair and a clear oval face. Her hairstyle was of the period, twisted around in an ornate bun at the back of her head — that much he noticed as she looked sharply at the young feller and himself. She wore a simple gingham dress in green and white checks. Wade was conscious of a lovely womanly body although she could not have been more than a few years older than the young hombre with the wounded shoulder.

An instant thought came to him that these two were brother and sister. They looked alike, some family resemblance — just a hunch he had.

“Why are you stopping him?” the girl cried. “I saw you through the window!”

Wade gave that slow grin of his. He

didn't know that it added a handsome twist to his taut, wary features.

"Ain't nothing much, young lady. Just happens I saw this young galoot when I was riding early this morn. I noticed he had stopped a bit of lead. I figured to help him but he fed steel to his horse and rode away. It's a wonder to me he made it into town. Did he get the wound seen to? Guess he must he hardy, huh?"

The girl held his glance for a moment and then lowered long-lashed eyes. "Tommy had an — accident. He's all right now. Thank you for thinking of helping him . . . "

"I'm going, Stella," muttered the young man. "Don't worry about me — and tell this stranger we don't need any help."

Wade grinned. "Obstinate young feller! Did you patch him up or did a doc do it?"

The lad called Tommy went along the boardwalk, reached a tie-rail and, gathering up the leathers of a bronc, leaped to the saddle and went off with only a curt glance at Wade Tulane.

"A doctor attended to Tommy, thank you," the girl said politely.

"Brother and sister, huh?" Wade flicked a glance at the gold lettering on the central window-pane of the store. He read the legend. W. CAMDEN. DRAPPER. He nodded to the sign. "That can't be you. Maybe you work here?"

"W.Camden was my father," said the girl quietly. "He's dead — only a few weeks ago. Anyone in Laredo can tell you that — if you're so curious . . . "

Wade Tulane replaced his hat. He slid the thong tight under his chin. "Sorry to hear that, young lady. In that case you ought to look after your brother. That lead in his shoulder could easily have been nearer his heart."

"Oh — I know!" She looked confused, as if with inner thoughts.

"You want any help?"

"I — I — I've got friends . . . "

"Sure — reckon a girl as pretty as

you will have friends." Wade gave a grim gesture to his guns. "These are my only friends in this town." He paused, thinking of Ezra Sloan. "Wal, almost my only pals . . . my name is Wade Tulane . . . I'm right now at the Bonanza Hotel an' if you need any help the offer still stands."

She looked at him uncertainly. He could almost read her mind. She was thinking he was a stranger in a town of hardcases. He could be any type — and he carried two guns.

Wade grinned. The smile wiped away the wary imprint on his face — and the girl noticed this change and gave a faint smile in return. "I'll know where to find you!" she gasped and turned and ran back into the drapery emporium.

Wade strolled away, grinning, a little bit enervated by the meeting with a lovely girl. There certainly had not been any such visions up in Colorado among the hardened gold-panners! He wondered if his offer to help the girl had been a wise one. Maybe he should be minding his own business.

All the same he had a feeling that this girl and her brother had a bit of trouble on their hands, but what that was he could barely guess at. Except one thing; the young feller had stopped a slug somewhere amid that grief!

Wade reached the Bonanza Hotel again, entered the lounge. Finding a leather armchair he slumped down, aware of some surge of the old tiredness. He tipped his hat over his eyes, slid down into the comfort of the chair and shut his eyes. The place held only two other men and they were confabbing, maybe over a business deal. Wade slid into sleep, and yet he could waken at a second's notice. Sleeping with two guns was a reminder that life could be hard. Still the armchair was better than a saddle and the movement of a bony animal under him. Sleep made his eyes heavy. Like an animal, he slumbered.

He came to instant alertness some ten minutes later when bawling voices arose in the air from outside the hotel. He knew it for a fight from the first second. Out of curiosity, he went to the nearest window and looked out.

Two men were slogging at each other and onlookers were already forming a circle around them, sending shouts and jeers into the air. Wade saw a youngish man in a black suit usually favoured by gamblers, doctors and mayors. He had a hunch that this struggling man was a gambler. He was opposed by another man who seemed a good fifteen years older, if iron-grey hair and a heavier body were any guide.

Hats lay in the dust. One black hat and one Stetson. Wade saw the older man step back, shrug out of his coat and hand it to someone in the crowd. Then the young gambler whipped out of his black coat, threw it down on the dusty ground and rushed in to renew the fight. Punches were hefted grimly as the men faced up to each other in the style of the old-time boxer.

Wade smiled slightly and figured he

might as well get a closer look. He liked a good scrap as well as the next guy.

He walked out of the hotel and crossed the boardwalk. He joined the circle of grinning and cheering onlookers. Somehow, within seconds, he found himself on the inside of the ring. The onlookers were eddying around so much that he didn't have to push forward.

The young gambler with the white vicious face was suddenly getting the worse part of the brawl, with ramming punches to the chin and eyes, and blood was spurting. Wade saw that and gave a shrewd glance at the older man, figuring him for a rancher because of that solid look and his clothes.

The fight was suddenly going bad for the gambler for he took plenty of slamming blows to the body and face. Dust kicked up from the road. Jeers and shouts went up from the assembled crowd but Wade could discover no reason for the rumpus. But reason there must be — probably some old enmity, some hatred.

The younger man crashed to the dusty ground and lay writhing and glaring. Then, gathering strength again, the mists in his brain probably vanishing, he scrambled to his feet. The older man seemed to hesitate, allowing the other time, a mistake in any fight. And so the young hombre rushed forward.

It seemed in those furious seconds that the young gambling man was intent on fisticuffs, but in a second the scene all changed. Wade saw the gambling-man's hand flash to his armpit. Wade realised in a flash, while the others around were shouting jeers, what was about to happen. Wade knew that the young gambler had a weapon hidden under that fancy vest.

The small derringer sprang into sight in the next moment and pointed grimly at the older man.

Wade had seen these shoulder-guns elsewhere. This was a typical gambler's idea. Usually a card-playing man gave the impression that he carried no guns, certainly not Colts. But a cunningly hidden weapon was typical of the type.

As the small pistol gleamed in the man's hand, Wade Tulane drew his Colt. It was a very fast draw, a split-second decision.

Wade's gun exploded just before the derringer barked its nasty little sound. Men scattered. The circle around the fighters widened and the shouts and jeers cut off like magic.

The gambling-man's little gun seemed to leap from his hand. Like a firework it jerked a few yards away to the ground, and left the man staring at his numbed hand.

In the silence that followed, the onlookers turned heads to stare at Wade Tulane. The tableau held for what seemed a long time in the evening light but in reality it was only seconds.

"Reckon that was a dirty trick tryin' to shoot a man in the middle of a fight," drawled Wade and he glanced around warily. "Sure hope you galoots figure it that way, too!"

A chorus of growls seemed to signify general assent, and the crowd began to break up, aware that the fight and entertainment was over. Wade watched the young gambling-guy take his black coat from a pal in the crowd and then bend down and pick up his small derringer. The man walked close to Wade Tulane.

Eyes glittered in a pale face as he sneered: "I'll remember you, pal."

"Sure hope so," drawled Wade, smiling but watching.

Wade Tulane slowly holstered his Colt without taking his eyes from the other. He stood and waited. Maybe it wasn't a good idea to turn his back and invite grief. It seemed the young gambler had pals in the crowd.

The older man who'd been fighting walked up and stuck out a hand in friendship. "Thanks. You maybe saved my life. Dave Latimer is the name . . . "

"Think nothing of it . . . " Wade smiled as he took the man's grip. He watched as a friend of Dave Latimer helped the man on with his browncoat and then handed him his gunbelt, which he strapped on. Not until all this was done was anything said. Then: "That Leo Sands is a young swine — but I figure I could have licked him . . . "

Wade grinned. "Yeah, I reckon. What was the trouble?"

"I warned him to keep away from a young gal called Stella Camden. He's pestering her to marry him . . . "

Wade suddenly realised with some wary, bitter feelings that he was getting into others' troubles right here in Laredo. With the events in Colorado still fresh in his mind, he wondered if this was wise. Trouble he could do without. Maybe in Colorado there were law officers who didn't believe the gunfight in Cactus Plain had been a fair one. Maybe he could still get trouble from that area. Maybe he should mind his own business in Laredo . . .

3

The Skunk

WADE moved slowly around on his heel. "I've met Miss Camden . . . a lovely gal . . . "

Surprise showed on Dave Latimer's face. "You have? I thought I knew all her friends. I'm by way of being her guardian since her pa died. Just like to help . . . "

Understanding of the cause of the fight came to Wade and he nodded. "I met Tommy Camden out in the desert. He was wounded and I figured he might fall from his cayuse — but it seems he's a hardy lad and made it back to town. Then I met up with him again beside the drapery store and Miss Stella came out. Ain't none of my business but I got a feeling those two have some trouble on their hands.

But maybe I should keep my nose out . . . "

A frown crossed Dave Latimer's face. His shrewd eyes appraised Wade Tulane, dropping down to the twin Colts slung in the gunbelt. Was this man a gunny pure and simple? A stranger, he decided, and Laredo was full of them and not all of them could be trusted. However this man had probably saved his life when he'd intervened in the fisticuffs.

So, speaking deliberately, watching Wade's face, he said: "William Camden, their father, was killed by a bushwhacker. He was a good man and a firm believer in the future of this town. He didn't like the rabble that has poured into the place, and he always hoped that the discovery of gold and the railroad and other big developments would bring progress to the town and not just grief. Then he was found in a canyon some seven miles east of Laredo, among the desert trails. There was a rifle bullet in his back. Bill Camden didn't tote a gun of any sort — never did. He called himself a trader and was against weapons, apart from hunting. I figure it kinda ironical that he should die like that . . . "

"Yeah . . . but who the hell would kill a gent like that?"

"The sheriff never found a damned thing worth two cents, so it is a complete blank. Nobody knows who killed Bill Camden — except the murderer — because that's what it was — murder! And we never figured out why William Camden was riding out through that desert canyon. He was mostly a townsman — never went far — "

"Guess all that is worrying Tommy and Stella," muttered Wade. "Still, ain't none of my business — I should remember that. But one last question: you got any idea who Tommy Camden has tangled with to deserve a slug in his shoulder?"

Dave Latimer frowned. "That I don't know. Maybe I ought to confab with that young feller."

Wade branched off on another kind of interrogation. "What's wrong with Leo Sands — apart from him being a gambler and a cuss?"

"Wrong!" exploded the other. "That jasper is all wrong for anybody — never mind a young gal who can have her choice of suitors in this town! Leo Sands is a skunk! Yessir! For a start he won't do any honest work and he drinks a lot — and, of course, gambles, that being his vocation, I'll allow. Sure, he usually wins. Aw, shucks, I've told him to keep away from Stella! He's no durned good for her. He is always askin' her to marry him — that cuss of a guy — marriage! He's a skunk."

"You say!"

"Wal, I do — and I don't care who hears me say it."

"That's why he was fighting with you!" observed Wade dryly.

"Sure. Marry that devil? Not if I can help it. I'll nail his hide to a barn door first!"

Wade figured that it was obvious that Dave Latimer and Leo Sands were complete enemies. He smiled and went on: "Are you a rancher?"

"Yep. Own the Cloverleaf down the valley. Ever you ride that way you'll be welcome to hitch up for the night."

"I'm Wade Tulane — bit of a wanderer, I guess."

"Two guns, I see. Not many pack that kind of hardware — sure invites trouble . . . "

"Or keeps it away." Wade grinned again. The other man noticed that the wary facial lines around his visage vanished in that grin. "I might try working a claim on the River Shasta — if I can find a spot worth claiming."

Dave Latimer nodded. "Those placer miners are sure gouging lumps out of the river — and panning like hell — but the real quartz is being mined in the hills. And you need heavy machinery for that, like rock-crushing gear."

Wade agreed. "Yeah. I'm not into that right now. Wouldn't mind panning some neat little nuggets out o' the river — but usually a man gets mostly dust."

"You've done some gold-panning?"

"Yep — in Colorado." Wade shut his mouth on that note and the other man noticed.

"If you need work I could fix you up if you can ride herd," muttered Dave Latimer.

"I'll think about it, Mister . . . "

"Call me Dave the next time you see me . . . "

They parted. Wade entered his hotel again and the rancher went on his way. Wade figured he would stand a better chance of a rest if he went up to his room and stretched out on his bed. If a man had any sense, he took rest when it came his way.

He eased off his boots, unbuckled his belt and looped it over the brass rail at the head of the bed. Suddenly it seemed a long time since he had last used a bed.

But he didn't go to sleep at once.

Instead he had a vision of Jack Rawkin as he had last seen him, falling to the ground, dead. Sure the other man had lost on the gunplay, that was all, but the scene in his mind's eye rankled. Wade had not wanted that. And the gold the double-crosser had taken was now lost, somewhere in Cactus Plain. Maybe the law had claimed it.

He had kept on riding. There'd be wanted posters outside lawmen's offices. The best he could hope for was that the affair would be forgotten in time along with the other violent acts of the West.

He had told Ezra Sloan the first yarn that had entered his mind. So far Ezra was the only one in Laredo who could connect him with Jack Rawkin.

He gradually relaxed . . . his eyes heavy with fatigue . . . but it was a sleep that held a wary instinct . . . the ability to be alert in a second . . . a man reaching for guns . . . if need be . . .

But nothing disturbed him. And the

darkness fell even deeper over the town and the lamps were lit at street corners. It was very late at night when Wade clawed his way out of the sleep that engulfed him. He got to his feet. There was some water in his room and he used it to dab his face and eyes. Then he strapped on his gunbelt again and thought he'd go down to the bar-room and take in a reviving drink of something strong.

When he stood against the polished counter, the place was filling up. Late hours were kept in frontier towns and in fact the middle of night was the most popular time — or until men got so drunk they just fell asleep where they sat.

There were groups of punchers and miners and some Irishmen from the railroad. Card-games were in progress. Staring over the haze of smoke from cigars, Wade saw Leo Sands at a table with three other men who, by their garb, seemed to be cowpokes.

Wade turned back to his glass of

Hermosilla beer. That Leo Sands should use the Bonanza Hotel as a place for his gambling was none of his business.

But the young gambling-man seemed bent on making himself unpleasant. As soon as he caught sight of Wade at the bar, he finished a hand, and then stood up with some muttered words to his companions. He strode over slowly, soft leather boots making his approach stealthy. Wade was aware of him at once and turned casually.

Wade's dark eyes flicked over the other's white face. Wade waited, thumbs hitched in his belt. He had not long to wait.

"I didn't like your play this afternoon," sneered Leo Sands. "You damned near shot a bit out of my hand. It's still numb . . . "

Wade could have ignored the statement of something which was now past and done, but he considered a warning should be handed to this upstart.

"Lay off me, mister. I carry two guns and I can use 'em. They ain't for show . . . "

It was a warning uttered so low that only the gambler could hear. Okay, Wade knew it was a boast. Two guns often were a boast. Wade could kill with one reliable Colt if need be — but in a contrary way he wasn't a killer. He was a guy living in the tough lawless West and guns meant defence as well as attack.

Leo Sands heard the warning. "I'm rememberin' you! You don't talk like that to me . . . "

"Then who the hell am I talking to? You just remember, pal, that I got two hoglegs. And I'm not the type to bushwhack easily."

Wade dropped his gaze momentarily. Okay, the other man did not wear any guns that were visible. But it was a good bet that his shoulder-holster was filled. Wade looked disdainfully at the man's fancy vest and he grinned without mirth.

"Why don't you button up, amigo?"

And with slow steady movements that were derisory, he reached out and twisted the two top buttons of the fancy vest into their respective button-holes. Leo Sands fumed, motionless, staring at Wade's hand, and then he acted, gripping the hand that mocked him.

"Cut it out!" It was a spit of low words, full of fury.

"Sure!" Wade laughed, and turned back to the bar counter and yet maintained a fixed encounter with the other's eyes.

Slowly, Leo Sands turned and walked away to his card-table, his bluff called and his hatred of Wade Tulane very real. Wade knew he had made an enemy. And it might not be funny. But he turned to his beer. Few in the bar-room had seen the incident because most of the saloon customers were arguing and confabbing loudly.

Wade realised one thing: Leo Sands was not the type who wanted to stage a gunfight on the time-honoured basis of the fast draw. He'd had the chance to face up and had backed down. Okay — but his quickly-formed hatred of Wade Tulane was forming into something very implacable. It might provoke him into a cowardly sly shot in a dark alley.

Wade got the feeling that the bar-room of the Bonanza Hotel was getting to be a bit crowded so he walked out. As he pushed through the doors into the night air, he did not see the bitter glance Leo Sands arrowed after him.

Wade went along the boardwalk, the night air cold after the warmth of the saloon. He was a big wary man in a dark shirt stretched tight across a wide chest. His boots clomped regularly on the boardwalk. Going on steadily, with no real destination except to take in some fresh air before he turned in for the night, to his surprise he was outside the little drapery emporium.

He halted. All at once he was

undecided. It was a novel experience for a man who usually went ahead rightly or wrongly on any project that was his concern.

He rolled a cigarette and lit up with a sulphur match. He stared at the glimmer of light that showed from somewhere inside the emporium. Noting that the front door seemed very solidly locked, and there was a shutter on the window, nevertheless the small emission of light seemed to suggest someone in the drapery store was still up at this time of night. Should he knock?

"Aw, shucks — who says that girl wants to be bothered with the likes of you?" he muttered to himself. As he hardly knew what was in his own mind, there was no answer to this question.

His narrowed eyes suddenly saw a burly man walking across the road. Yellow light from a nearby saloon showed the star pinned to the man's long-tailed black coat. It seemed that this was the sheriff maybe a guy to be wary of!

Wade instinctively tensed and then he relaxed with a bitter smile as the other man mounted the boardwalk. There was a time when he could have walked past any sheriff without a worry — but not since the death of Jack Rawkin. Damn that robbing so-called friend!

In the half-light the sheriff could not have seen him properly. It was unlikely the man was looking for him, anyway, so why should he tense up so much! But the sheriff came quite close. Before he halted outside the door of the drapery store he flashed a glance at Wade but it meant nothing. Then, looking away again, the sheriff knocked on the door of the drapery shop. So he'd been heading for the place! Wade kept on propping up the wall. He was close enough to see the features of the lawman even in the yellow half-light from a nearby street lantern.

Then the emporium door opened and a shaft of oil-lamp light fell out over the boardwalk. Wade got a swift impression of Stella Camden's sweet but dismayed face and the stern look on the heavy features of the sheriff — and then he heard talk.

"I don't like to do this, Miss Stella, but I got to see that brother of yourn. Reckon he's at home, huh?"

"I — I — why do you want to see him, Sheriff Hapner?"

"You ought to know, Miss Stella," said the sheriff flatly. "He's been in a shootin' affair and what's more the body of Mac Heggety was found out in the desert country beside the buttes. Now I reckon to talk with that brother of yourn, Miss Stella . . . "

"He's — he's — not here!" gasped the girl, and she tried to slam the door in the lawman's face.

The man was an old hand at this sort of treatment and his boot was in the doorway practically at the same time that the girl slammed the door. She struggled to keep the sheriff out, but with one hefty push the indignant lawman rammed the door back, making the hinges shudder.

"That ain't the way to treat Bill Hapner," he barked. "Now where's that young fool! I want to parley with him."

His request was a bit late. Wade Tulane and the sheriff heard the rapid tattoo of hoofs from the alley behind the store and guessed the rest. Smiling faintly, Wade guessed that Tommy Camden was getting out the only way he knew how — and that was by way of a fast horse! But that kind of play only pointed the finger of guilt at him, the young fool!

Sheriff Bill Hapner swung back from the store doorway and leaped down the boardwalk in order to get a better view of the departing horseman. There was only a momentary view of a dark shape on a galloping horse and the drum of hoofs on the hard earth and then the rider flung the animal around a corner and was gone.

Wade noticed the sheriff had drawn a gun, but he had not cocked the hammer. Maybe it was just a gesture on the part of the lawman. Maybe he was reluctant to shoot.

Bill Hapner swung his burly frame around and glared at the girl in the doorway. "Crazy young idjut! I reckon he killed Mac Heggety!"

"It was a fair fight," cried the girl. "And Mac Heggety and his cowardly brother Rip killed my father! We know they did! It's true . . . "

"Wal, I don't know. You need proof, young lady. And Tommy shouldn't take the law into his own hands. And won't do him any good to light out of town."

"You just scared him," returned the girl. "He won't take to the owlhoot trail — he'll come back. Give him time, Sheriff Hapner."

"Where's he likely to head for?" barked the sheriff.

"I wouldn't know . . . "

"Sure getting to be a mighty lawless town," grumbled Bill Hapner, and then he glanced across at Wade. "What in heck are you doing skulking there?"

Wade walked forward. "Reckon I was about to call on Miss Camden when you moseyed up."

"At this time o' night, hombre?"

"Yeah — it is late — but I saw a light."

"Who are you?"

"Wade Tulane, Sheriff. A stranger in town." Wade watched the other's reaction, but the name seemed to mean nothing.

"Guess they are all strangers in town right now," snapped the lawman, and he stepped down from the boardwalk. "I'm aiming to look for Tommy," he continued warningly. "And I want to know the truth about Mac Heggety. An' take my advice, Miss Stella, don't go around saying Mac and Rip killed your pa if you can't prove the words. Mac is sure dead — in the mortuary right now with the town undertaker looking at the cadaver — but Rip Heggety is very much alive and a real mean cuss at the best of times."

And with that final word the sheriff tramped away, bent upon his business, a disgruntled man.

Wade Tulane smiled and turned to the girl. "Seems your brother, Tommy, is in trouble. Well, if it ain't none of my business, just say so. Then I'll be on my way . . . " Wade reflected that he seemed destined to get mixed up in all kinds of dangerous events.

Lamplight gleamed on her pretty face, revealing her anxiety. "You again, Mr Tulane! Oh, I've heard all about you . . . "

"All?"

"How you helped Dave Latimer in that fight."

"Just did what the others would have done if they'd got around to it."

"I hate Leo Sands!" She nearly stamped her foot and then looked confused. "Nothing would ever make me marry him! Or even think about him in — in — that way! I know you've heard about that from Dave Latimer — he came along to have a talk with Tommy."

Wade moved closer to the girl but half turned so that he could scan the empty poorly-lit street. A rider came past. The man was probably some cowboy riding in late for entertainment, but Wade had another surge of inbred wariness and felt safer with his back to a wall. So he hardly understood his motives when he heard himself saying, "I'd like to help you, Miss Stella . . . I'm nothing but a wanderer and you can tell me to shooshay if you figure it ain't none of my business, but killing is a serious affair even in a boom-town like this with very little law. Tommy might have a posse after him pretty soon if he don't come back and explain."

The girl hesitated. Wade went on: "Mind you, the sheriff might not be able to get possemen. Not every galoot wants to go riding out with a gun for nothing . . . ”

To his surprise the girl asked swiftly: “Have you got a horse ready?”

“I could fork the crittur,” he admitted. “Why?”

“Get your horse, Mr Tulane, and come back here for me.”

“Sure is late,” he began, “and my horse has had a hard time — but I’ll do it.”

“I’ll change from this dress into something suitable for riding. Perhaps you can help me find Tommy — now — tonight. I have a feeling I know where he’ll be. Will you help me? You said you would help.”

Wade smiled in spite of his reservations about attracting attention in this part of Texas. “I’m a hombre with an idle loop,” he admitted. “I’ll help you. I’ll go get my horse . . . ”

He strode away and heard the door shut behind him. He walked along, tiredness forgotten, with long purposeful strides, past the Bonanza

Hotel and the La Belle saloon, from where sounds of drunken merriment still emanated and came to the livery where he had left his horse.

He noted that the old hostler was still there, asleep on a bale of straw, and Wade told the man curtly to rub down the black horse and get the animal ready. Then Wade swiftly went to his hotel, into his room, and carried out his saddle-gear. He left his rifle in the room, considering that Colts were sufficient to carry. He walked through the bar on his way out to the street.

He was not thinking about Leo Sands and so he did not see the gambling-man eyeing him narrowly as he carried the saddle-gear to the batwings and out into the street.

Wade saddled up in the livery and thought that the animal was fairly rested and so a short ride would do little harm. He led the horse out of the livery and handed the old wrangler some money for his recent attentions to the animal, and then he swung up into the saddle. He jigged the horse down the street and then dismounted beside the drapery store.

Stella Camden had changed swiftly. When he heard the sound of a horse in the alley at the side of the clapboard store, he turned and stared.

"Which way do we go?" he asked.

She pointed down the street, to the east of the town. "We'll ride that way. I think we'll find Tommy. The sheriff is right — we must try to explain that it was a fair fight between Mac Heggety and Tommy."

Wade swung back to his saddle and rode down the street with the girl, stirrup to stirrup. She had changed into jeans which were tucked into riding-boots, and she wore a buckskin jacket of Indian handiwork. A small blue hat almost hid her fair hair but some wisps hung down over her eyes. This much Wade saw in the light of a street lantern which they passed at a corner and then they were in the darkness again. For some moments they rode in silence. It was enough that he had volunteered to help; she could explain something about her situation in her own good time.

It was only a matter of minutes of riding and they were almost out of Laredo, leaving the straggle of cabins and the stockyards that marked the outskirts of the town. The only light on the well-rutted trail east out of the town came from a pale moon which had started to emerge from a break in the clouds.

"Mac Heggety and his brother Rip killed my father," she suddenly began to explain in a low voice. "But I can't prove that. Perhaps I should tell you everything, Mr Tulane. I feel I can confide in you . . . "

"Sure like to hear you say that," admitted Wade. "You can start by calling me by my first name. Never could get used to anyone calling me Mister . . . "

In the darkness, as they rode slowly,

he heard her laugh musically, and he knew she was a warm human being. Strangely, he wanted to know her better.

"All right — Wade. Frankly, sometimes the conventions bore me — or should I not dare say that! So please call me Stella . . . "

He leaned on the saddle-horn. "It's a mighty bad thing that your father was killed. Dave Latimer told me a bit about him. Now if you'll excuse a straight question, why should anyone want to kill your pa? Don't you have some ideas?"

"He was bushwacked," said Stella angrily. "He never carried guns and he was shot down in the back — which makes it a skunk's doing. As to your question, Wade — Tommy and I don't know at all why anyone should want to kill our pa. He never harmed anyone, and I never thought he had enemies. That is until after he was killed — and then we began to suspect Mac Heggety and his younger brother, Rip. It's so hard to explain why we're sure they killed Pa, but those two came to the store and offered to buy the place one day. We told them we didn't want to sell. You'd have thought that rebuff would have been sufficient, but practically every few days they returned and made offers that gradually became crazy.

"What do you mean by that?"

"They offered more for the store than it is worth lock, stock and barrel!" cried the girl.

"Seems queer. They don't seem the type to pay over the odds for anything, from what you have told me . . . "

"And that's not all. Tommy caught them one night rifling through the house at the back of the store. Tommy had taken me to a concert at the church hall and we'd returned perhaps a bit early because one of the performers did not turn up and the concert was quickly over."

"Yeah?" Wade was puzzled.

"Tommy and I went into the store

from the front door — there is a door at the back which serves the house, and there is an enclosed yard and stable. Tommy saw men moving in the living-room and a light was on. Well, he dashed forward. He wasn't wearing a gun. He is actually too young to walk around like a gun-toting hardcase. He — "

The girl saw the rueful look on Wade's face and, laughingly, she laid a hand on his arm, reaching across from her horse to do it.

"I didn't quite mean it that way! I know you carry guns! But you know what I mean. You'll agree that Tommy is just a youth and, anyway, our pa did not encourage him to handle guns. But he did, of course — like most young men around these parts he wanted to be a great shot — and I know he practised secretly. Well, that is all by the way. Tommy was not wearing a gun when he dashed into the living-room after those two men . . . "

"Two men, Stella?"

"Yes, two of them. But they were quick. They got out very fast and they had horses in the alley. They just raced away at full lope. We couldn't do anything to stop them. When we looked around the house we found it had been ransacked. Tommy and I thought it very strange that some money had not been taken. Then we found a lantern the two men had left behind. It had the initials 'M.H.' scratched on one side."

"Mac Heggety?"

"That's what we thought. We told the sheriff. We went with him to the placer claim that the two Heggety brothers worked on the river. But they practically laughed in our faces and denied that the lantern belonged to them. The sheriff couldn't prove anything — not that he tried very hard. The initials happened to fit two other men — one in town and the other a placer miner. So we came away and had to forget the whole thing — not that we did!

But we knew who had killed Pa — Mac Heggety and Rip! It was just one of those sure hunches — so hard to explain and yet founded on instinct!"

4

The Fight

THERE was silence between Wade and the girl for some moments as they rode along the trail, the unexpected moonlight helping them find a way along the hard-packed ground.

Wade looked at the girl again, something he found pleasure in doing. "Hmmm — from what you've said it ain't likely that your father was bushwacked for nothing. By that I mean the breaking into your house and ransacking means there is some kind of crazy reason for the actions of these two rannigans."

"Only one now," Stella reminded him. "And that's Rip Heggety." Wade thought he detected some satisfaction in her voice.

"Yep. One has bitten the dust," he chuckled. "I hope your brother can prove it was a fair fight — " He broke off thinking that a fair fight didn't always clear the survivor. "Guess we'll have to find him — where do you figure he's gone? I reckon you are riding this trail for some solid reason . . . "

"Yes, I have an idea where he's gone," said the girl, and she urged her animal into a canter where the terrain was flat and easy. "And that's why I've asked you to help. You're the man with the guns . . . "

"So you've noticed," said Wade dryly.

"Oh, I mean it in the nicest way! And I'm sure you won't really have to fire them! I feel sure that Tommy has headed for the River Shasta — to get hold of Rip Heggety and make him confess. He was hinting that when Sheriff Hapner knocked on our door."

"That ain't such a healthy idea," muttered Wade. "I'm more than darned sure that this Rip galoot is a hardcase of the first order and getting him to confess anything will be some job. Anyway Tommy is not too far ahead of us — unless he's feeding spurs to that cayuse of his. And that's what he's probably doing right now. But it's a dangerous ride in this half-light and man could get thrown from his horse."

"We might catch up," said the girl, but there was some doubt creeping into her remark.

They rode faster until the ground became rough and the moon disappeared for some minutes. The more Wade Tulane thought about this ride out the more he realised that Tommy Camden had a good point if he could get Rip Heggety to admit guilt. If the man could be made to admit that he and his brother had killed Stella's father — but that was a tall order! How could that be done? Some sort of force would be needed. The force behind a gun?

Making a man like this Rip Heggety

confess guilt would need Colt action — that was the way Wade saw it. Sure, if it could be proved to the law that the Heggety brothers had killed the father then the man who killed Mac Heggety would be in the clear.

But the law and gunplay was often fraught with problems, as Wade had discovered. And how could Tommy Camden, a youngster just into his teens, achieve all this?

The trail twisted around some big buttes and then led through a plain dotted with scrub trees and some cactus. The moonlight threw a wan illumination over the rough country. After a mile or so of this, Wade noticed the land freshed with grass and the greedy cholla cactus, and then they entered a gully which led right down to the side of a fair-sized stream, which he knew must be the River Shasta. He had not seen the land before but this was undoubtedly the terrain of which men spoke.

As they rode along under the moon,

now blessedly giving some light, the girl still leading the way, he speculated on the chain of events that had got him into helping this girl.

It wasn't a very strong chain and he could back out easily — but strangely he didn't want to double-track in this way. Not on any account, something he could not analyse within himself. He was not an impressionable man — and he was not without cares — he had the new fear of being challenged as wanted man, although he couldn't be sure events had taken that trail. Maybe he should mind his own business, backtrack while he had time, because possibly he was riding into a queer tangle.

All at once the ride brought them to the first of the placer mining camps, a familiar scene to Wade Tulane. The sight of lights near tents brought back memories of Jack Rawkin and the camp they shared in Colorado. A tight wary look settled on his face and he became silent — and the girl noticed.

Lights and fires, near to tents and ramshackle cabins, studded the river bank, although it was late night and some of the miners had finished working for the day and were carousing. The sound of strong-voiced men cursing and arguing and laughing came to his ears and he wondered at the wisdom of riding this way with a girl. Horses whinnied somewhere near a clump of trees along with the sound of someone hammering away, metal on metal. As they rode along the trail he wondered if it was not time he took the lead. He patted his Colt gun, instinctively, in the holster, a reassuring action. This was a place where trouble could whip up fast. And where the heck was Tommy Camden?

Wade rode abreast of the girl's pinto. "Do you know where this hellion, Rip Heggety, has his claim?"

"Yes, of course. It's at the end of this camp, by a big growth of willows." She pointed through the night air.

He nodded. "Reckon I'll go first,

Stella. What is your main intention? Just to get Tommy back to town and out of trouble?"

"I suppose that's the idea — unless he has made Rip Heggety talk — in which case I'd love to haul that devil back to the sheriff."

Wade made warning sounds. "That's a tough assignment for a young feller — and even tougher for you, Stella! Do you understand the dangers? These men are rough swines . . . "

"You think I'm being foolish!" she challenged.

"No. But some tasks are too much for a girl, no matter how high-spirited. And Tommy could be in grief any moment now . . . "

It seemed a startlingly prophetic remark, for as they jigged the horses up to the clump of willows a din of bawling voices broke out. There was a slither of boots on shale and then hoarse gasps and yells as men exchanged blows.

It was enough for Wade. "Wait

here!" he said sharply to the girl. He did not pause to see if she obeyed but urged his mount forward and went down the slight incline to the edge of the river in a rapid rataplan of hoofs on gravel and stones.

At the end of the ride he slid from his horse and strode towards two men who fought savagely as they pounded blows at each other in a rough and tough whirl of fists. Wade had seen Tommy Camden. He was undoubtedly getting the worst of the fight in the few seconds that elapsed as he wondered if he should allow them to fight it out. It was little wonder that the youngster fell back. The other hell-raiser, who was presumably Rip Heggety, had slammed a wicked, low punch into the lad's guts. Granted that this was a brawl, it was still a vicious blow — and the man followed it up.

Tommy Camden staggered and fell to the ground. The other rushed up and crouched for a leap. Wade knew what was coming. He had seen that rough-house trick many times. Rip Heggety figured to jump down on his opponent's body — probably the face — with all the force of a miner's steel-studded boots!

Wade shot in, head down like a battering-ram, just as Rip Heggety leaped. The two collided, but not over the body of Tommy Camden for he had sensed what was coming and had rolled!

Wade Tulane's hatted head rammed into Rip Heggety's belly and stopped the man completely. Actually, he staggered back and fell to earth, his boots thudding into the gravel and shale. Wade lost his hat, not that he noticed that little detail. He advanced to the prone man.

Stella had not been wrong when she had hinted that Rip Heggety was a rough, tough young hellion. In spite of his severe impact with the ground, he scrambled up again to meet Wade.

His boots dug at the earth. One moment he was prone — and then with vicious speed he was charging his opponent, hissing with an animalistic fury. Wade got a glimpse of a contorted visage that might at any other time, in calmer mood, be considered handsome in a reckless way. The rough-house man was dressed in a dirty checked shirt, with pants tucked into heavy boots. Obviously, he was no dandy of the town.

"I'll smash you, stranger!" he roared. "Then I'll beat this pup to a pulp so that he won't hell around killin' other men!"

His arms were milling savagely as he closed in.

Wade had time to reflect that Rip Heggety knew about his brother's death. He wondered how long he'd known this fact. Not long, he figured. Sheriff Hapner had just started on an investigation — so that meant the body had just been brought in. As Hapner had hinted, the cadaver was in the town morgue.

Wade's flash of thought terminated

as the other man slammed out a fist that had the force of a swinging shovel. Wade hardly knew how to dodge it, but he did in a swift reaction. Grimly, he realised he would have to bring all his strength to a peak if he wanted to beat this hellion. Momentum brought Rip Heggety close to him and Wade got a grim impression of a savage. Wade slammed in his first blow, a right-handed swing that crashed into the other's face. At least he had scored with this brute!

It was the first of a series of blows by both relentless men and at the start of this barrage of savagery Rip Heggety had some advantage because of his sheer animalism. Then Wade made a new effort to match a crazed man, a physical retaliation he had not made in any encounter with another man for a long time. Hoarse gasps were belted out of each man as they slammed into each other, boots slithering on loose shale as the two fighters staggered around on the rough terrain.

Wade fought grimly, coldly, realising this guy was no soft-living man. Each blow brought blood to each man. Some swinging punches missed, but the two were at it again in seconds. Wade had slammed in punches in a style that would have been approved in a roped ring, but continuing this style of fighting was not Rip Heggety's idea of beating an enemy. He wanted sheer savagery.

He suddenly charged in again and grappled with Wade. He swung Wade off his feet with the sheer fury of his charge and the two men crashed to the earth.

If Rip Heggety had expected to get the upper hand out of the fall, he was disappointed, for Wade rolled grimly the moment his back rasped into the shale ground. He jerked the other man around and grabbed at his hands, seeking to stop the huge paws that brutally sought his neck.

Wade got a ramming fist into Rip Heggety's face and felt the warm red blood spurt. The other writhed like a roped steer. It seemed impossible to keep this savage man down but Wade managed to do that for a while. Wade slammed another deadly blow into the contorted bloodied face while Heggety wasted his chances in trying to throw Wade off his body. The last blow dazed Heggety. Wade grabbed him by the long hair and his shirt and lifted the hellion up about a foot. Then he crashed him down again, the man's head ramming sickeningly against some rock. If the other blow had momentarily dazed Rip Heggety, this last treatment left him semiconscious. Wade Tulane repeated the harsh process. A certain amount of brutality was needed with a roughneck like Rip Heggety, because the man himself would deal out even worse punishment given half a chance. In fact he would kill . . .

Wade twice crashed the rannigan's head against the ground, and he felt the man's body go limp and his hands fall uncertainly. It seemed that Rip

Heggety was out of this world . . .

Wade got up — a mistake. As he crouched over the man, sure enough the brute strength in Rip Heggety returned, like a rage, and with a clearer mind threw him back into the battle. But Wade had the upper hand in that he was on his feet, perfectly balanced, breathing heavily and bleeding. As he saw the other endeavour to rise, he slammed a terrible punch to the man's chin. Rip Heggety fell back with a snarling moan.

But he even tried once more. He rolled suddenly after he had lain still for some moments, like a man feigning death, and then as Wade crouched the man's feet lashed out with heavy boots. Wade jerked back, avoiding the threshing boots, and then he rammed more terrible blows to the other's head. Rip Heggety slumped, beaten at last. Wade straightened, shoved his hand to his gun and glared around.

There were onlookers in the darkness; men near a tent; another, thumbs hooked in a belt, staring at the brawlers.

And yet another holding a horse. It was photographic impression that told Wade these men showed no sign of intervening or going for a gun.

Rip Heggety stirred again and sat up, barely conscious, unaware of what was going on, his brain full of mists. He did not attempt to start fighting again, but in accepting the beating he glared at the man who had licked him. He did not go for his gun because that would be to invite a slug. Maybe he decided there would be a better time and a better place in which to resort to guns. Anyway, he was in no condition to attempt a fast draw.

Wade Tulane backed staggeringly towards his horse, pain hitting him, blood on his face, a red mist in his eyes. He suddenly realised the best thing was to get Tommy Camden back to Laredo and safety.

Incongruously, Wade stopped and picked up his hat. Rip Heggety stood up and swayed, bracing his shoulders and wiping blood and sweat from his bruised face.

"I'll remember you, stranger!" The voice-thickened challenge was a real threat.

It was the second time an enraged man had said that to Wade Tulane since he had entered Laredo. There was nothing funny in a man adding to his enemies. Wade felt a deadly grimness about the whole thing. Was he a fool to go on making enemies?

He sensed that Tommy and his sister were further up the slope. Probably Tommy had collected his horse . . .

All at once, like a changing drama, Wade heard the rapid thud-thud of hoofs on the hard ground, and turning in grim alertness he was in time to see Tommy Camden urging his horse into a frantic forward movement.

Someone shouted: "The sheriff!"

It was indeed. And with the sheriff was another man who seemed to be a deputy. They thundered down the rocky trail in the half-light of the moon, slowing only momentarily to take in the scene, and the next instant they were off in pursuit of Tommy Camden.

Wade cursed again under his breath, This young fool was only making matters worse by once more taking to flight. Wade grabbed his horse, jigged it up the slope until he hit the trail, and there he was joined by the girl. She stared fearfully at the vanishing riders. "The sheriff is after him! What shall we do?"

Then she saw the blood on Wade's face. "You're hurt!"

"Wal, that ain't nothing," he stated. "We'll have to ride after Tommy. If Hapner catches the young idiot, we want to be on hand to explain a bit. C'mon . . . "

He lightly touched his horse with the rowels and the animal responded by springing into a full lope. The horseflesh was game, especially after the hard work the critter had done on the trail to Laredo and the lack of rest. As for himself Wade thought, he was in the same state as his horse — plumb tuckered out with fighting, with activity, lack of rest and too much tension — but he figured he'd jest go along. It wasn't the first time he had suffered a hard trail!

Stella's mount moved quickly, too, and it was just as well they went off fast for a gun barked from the direction of Rip Heggety's camp. The bullet whistled harmlessly through the night air, however, for Wade and the girl were quick-moving targets.

They urged their animals away from the placer camp, following the river-bank trail. Camp-fires spaced the river at almost regular intervals and they could see the dark shapes of men, not that they were working. Panning for gold was over for the day and the night, although some characters with the urge for gold were known to work by lantern-light! But the night was taking over and tired men were thinking of blankets.

Little notice was taken of their swift ride. Sometimes reckless riders pushed animals this way, in some sudden urgency, but this bunch of men were taking no notice.

After pursuing a mile or so of the rough trail in the uncertain light of a clouded moon, they encountered two riders sitting astride blowing horses. These men were the sheriff and his deputy, a man Wade had never seen before, and they seemed really angry.

Sheriff Bill Hapner recognised Stella and Wade in the gloom. "He got away, that brother of yourn! This trail forks and by heck we went down the wrong one for a few hundred yards before I figured it out."

"We'll find him again, sheriff" the girl shouted back. "And we'll clear up everything. Tommy only ran off to this camp to make Rip Heggety confess that he and his brother had killed my father. If Mac Heggety was the murderer of my father, that fact would clear Tommy, wouldn't it? I mean, that would be justice!"

"You're still toting that yarn!" barked the man. "How many times have I got to tell you that I want proof. Mac and Rip Heggety had alibis the day your pa was killed!"

"Their ruffian pals would say anything for a bottle of rot-gut," shouted the girl.

"Maybe. But I haven't any proof that them two devils killed your pa — only wish I had, Miss Stella. Anyway your brother has salivated Mac Heggety out in the desert — and that's got to be investigated. Gawd, the grief this town is giving me! Maybe I should retire!"

"They had a fair fight. They both drew guns. Tommy was wounded — we all know that — but it wasn't too bad."

"Don't stop him riding away like a fool!" snapped the sheriff. "Maybe it was a fair fight — I dunno — and you didn't see it, Miss Stella. The young fool — he's just making things worse for himself by running away."

"He's young — and — inexperienced, sheriff. He wasn't brought up to deal with gun-toters. And he's scared a bit, I'm sure . . . "

"Yep, by heck he ought to be! I'd like to hear him explain how come he just happened to be close to Mac Heggety out on the desert trail near the buttes! Seems mighty like he was trailin' Heggety." The sheriff spat saliva to the dust. "Durn it — how do I know it was a fair fight? Maybe Tommy jumped the other hombre and got that slug in his shoulder for fair exchange!"

"Maybe you could give the young galoot the benefit of the doubt," put in Wade smoothly.

"Not if I can prove murder. I'm not handing favours to any guy in this town. All hellions are treated the same . . . "

"Tommy isn't a hellion!" shouted the girl.

"Wal, it's gettin' mighty lawless without me encouraging men to go killin' each other."

Wade Tulane smile thinly, the gloom and his Stetson hiding his fleeting expression. He had a sudden hunch that sheriff Bill Hapner's bark was worse than his bite! But he did not doubt that the lawman was a stickler for duty and justice.

"Guess you know that Miss Stella and Tommy caught two hombres ransacking their house just after Mr Camden was killed and they figured them for the Heggety brothers."

"Yep. I know that. But nobody caught those men red-handed. I could spend a lot of time pinning things on men without proof. Say, you aiming to be an unpaid deputy?"

"Wal, you could say I'm giving a hand . . ."

"Why in heck? Stranger, ain't you? Wade Tulane, huh! I got your name — if it means anything and it's your real name. Plenty men around here just pick up any monicker."

Wade tightened his expression and

wondered if the name was going to strike the sheriff as something significant. Maybe he should have adopted another name when he had hit Laredo — like many a desperado, as the sheriff had hinted.

But he wasn't a desperado. And he had met one person who knew his real name — Ezra Sloan! Might have been hard explaining a change of title!

"Don't you figure there was something mighty strange about two men ransacking William Camden's house so soon after his death?" questioned Wade.

Sheriff Hapner fingered his bristly moustache. "Sure, sure. It's a bit odd, I'll allow — and if you can find real explanations, hombre, I'll be sure glad to listen . . . "

Wade leaned on his saddle-horn. "I don't know the answer any more than you do, but maybe I'll find some facts. To my mind Tommy and Stella haven't had the right sort of help to discover what is going on. Seems very strange to me that the Heggety men offered to buy the drapery store for more than it's worth. What do you make of that, Sheriff? Then two rannigans — two, mark you — ransack the house — so what the devil were they looking for?"

"I don't know, Tulane," snapped the other man. "Let me tell you I got a mighty lawless town on my hands and it ain't easy with killings and robberies almost every day. I can't deal with everything. Maybe I should look into your identity, for instance! Yeah — you see, it's difficult. I've been talking to the mayor about more deputies but he objects to the durned cost and says the taxes won't stand it. Heck, I don't know why I don't just buy me a ranch and mind my own business. If I had the dinero, I'd do that mighty fast!"

Wade smiled. Then the highly-incensed lawman turned his horse. "We're hitting the trail back to town and git some shut-eye. It's too durned late and too durned dark to achieve anything." He flung a glance at the girl. "You can save me a lot of trouble by bringing that young idiot brother of yourn in for questioning. In any case, he'd be safer in the jail because Rip Heggety is going to be meaner than mountain-cat. I don't think it has sunk in that Mac Heggety is real dead. Aw, he knows the truth — but given more time he'll be real mad. He'll go for guns, Miss Stella. He'll aim to kill your brother! Aw, why do I have to be a John Law!"

With this disgusted comment, the sheriff spurred his horse forward, his silent deputy following him down the trail. Wade jigged his black close to the girl's pinto. "The sheriff is about right . . . Rip Heggety will be plenty mad . . . that rough jasper is bad medicine. Your brother is in a spot . . . "

Stella stared around the terrain in the semi-darkness. There was desperation in her voice. "We've got to find Tommy. We've got to prove to the sheriff it was a fair fight . . . "

"Easier said than done," murmured Wade.

The girl cried out, "We've got to protect Tommy until Rip Heggety cools down."

"If he does. That kind of man will nurse an instinct for revenge for a long time."

There was silence as the horses picked slowly ahead. Then: "Let's get going," muttered Wade. "We're too near the mining camps for our health. Some of these men might be pally with Heggety." He paused. "I guessed your Tommy is a little impulsive, huh? He should have known he hadn't a coyote's chance of making a man like Heggety confess to anything! He's dealing with a mean galoot! And don't forget that Tommy still has a wounded shoulder — it must be giving him some pain. Yeah — a headstrong young feller, if nothing else."

"Are you regretting helping us?" asked the girl faintly.

"Nope. Just ruminating . . . "

"I've dragged you into our troubles," said Stella. She tried to laugh. "And frankly there isn't any real reason why you should tangle with men like Heggety just for our sakes. I wouldn't blame you if you stopped helping us."

Wade smiled faintly. It was a strange mixture of shyness and a quirky twist of the lips, something that made him attractive to the ladies — but he did not realise that!

"It isn't quite like that, Miss Stella," he drawled. "I'm a hombre on the loose. I ain't so handy with words — but I wouldn't back down from helping you now if there were ten hell-bents like Rip Heggety out there."

His explanation was not quite correct! He had a definite urge to help this slender, fair-haired girl because he had a strong desire to know her better! He'd encountered women in his life but not one with the beautiful innocence of Stella Camden and this quality appealed to some need deep inside him.

They rode down the trail, away from the river bank. There was little sign out here of men's activities, no mining or camps, only the moon made some illumination. Great cacti with thick straggly trunks took on the appearance of weary old skeletons in the pale light. Here and there he saw clumps of mesquite and catclaws looking like pleasant green bushes and not grim thorny plants that could tear a man to bits.

Moonlight on the semi-arid land is a mystical experience for most travellers, and there was a curious feeling of unreality about the ride back. Wade had to remind himself that they were seeking a young guy who was, at the moment, hiding from the law — and sought by a ruffian wanting revenge. That was a grim mix!

They trotted on a portion of the trail that allowed faster travel. They could not look for sign in this light.

Wade had the feeling they were on a wild-goose chase.

Then as they rounded a hulking rocky sentinel, a voice called out to them.

"Sis! I'm here!"

5

"Say Your Prayers!"

WHEN he realised that Wade and the girl were not accompanied by the sheriff and his deputy, Tommy rode out to meet them. He jigged his brown mare from out of the cover of the huge rock and in some moments they made a little group.

"You sure helped me out of that mess, Tulane," said the young fellow frankly. "Dave Latimer spoke well of you, too. That was when he called to ask how come I'd got a wound. Maybe I'm a fool, Tulane. I couldn't have beaten Rip Heggety with my shoulder the way it is. It damn-well still hurts — even with a bandage on it."

"Your best plan is to get back to town — "

"And have the sheriff clap me in jail," interrupted the young lad. "And maybe Rip Heggety come gunning for me?"

"I got a hunch you can talk the sheriff into accepting your account of the shooting-match between you and Mac Heggety," said Wade abruptly. He glanced at the girl. "Hapner is the law around here . . . "

"And what about Rip? I couldn't face up to that hellion with guns. I've heard he's fast."

"I'll see you don't have to draw against Rip Heggety," snapped Wade.

"You mean that?" gulped the young fellow. "Hell I admit I'm scared, the more I think about it! I've been an idiot. I can't match Heggety — and I don't know why I thought I could tangle with him. I'm not cut out for this kind of hellin' around, Tulane. Maybe you don't know, but I work on the Laredo Journal, a kind of reporter, just gathering bits of news for old Ben Smith, my boss. I don't work in the drapery store — not much. Anyway, writing bits of news isn't the kind of work that fits me for tackling men like Rip Heggety."

"You tackled his brother," said Wade. He searched the other's eyes. "I'd like to hear your account of that gunplay. How did you manage to kill that man, Tommy? Give me some straight answers. Why were you out in the desert lands at the same time and the same place. How did you beat him with a gun?"

"I'll tell you, Tulane," muttered the other. "Just like I told Stella — and Dave Latimer when he called. I rode into Mac Heggety by pure accident. I didn't trail him. And you know where I first sighted him?"

"Where?"

"He was ridin' mighty strangely through the canyon where our pa was found dead!"

"Yeah? How come you were there, too?"

"Just chance! I got the urge to ride

through that place and as I had some free time I saddled up and rode along. I never expected to see Mac Heggety there. I was simply moseying around, I guess, obeying some queer urge to look at the place. I've always wondered why Pa was out of town the day he got that damn bushwack bullet, because he never travelled much. I wanted to ride through the canyon just to figure out some hunches why Pa was out there the day he died. And then I came across Mac Heggety. You know he was a good many years older than Rip — and with more cunning than sheer roughness — not that I ever had much to do with these rannigans in the usual way, but as a reporter gathering news I heard many stories.

"Anyway, Mac Heggety was riding slowly and stopping every few yards to examine the canyon wall . . . "

"Mighty strange," murmured Wade.

"Yeah — I watched him for some time and then my horse neighed. Heggety then jerked like he had been caught out doing somethin' he shouldn't be at — if that makes sense to you. It was a bit mysterious — and I wasn't backing down — so I just sat my cayuse as he rode up."

"When did you shoot?"

"Believe me I never thought I'd be pushed into gunplay! He just rode towards me across that canyon floor — and then I realised he was itching to go for his hardware. I just knew the signs . . . "

"Yeah, I know the feeling. And?"

"As I say, he rode up, slowly, staring like a hawk at me — all tensed, his hand hovering over his gun-butt. Not a darned word issued from him — but it was sheer confrontation. And then — "

"Yeah?"

"His hand shot like a clamp over the gun-but and whipped out the smokepole. But his very attitude was like some sort of magnet to me — and my gun was out as fast as his! I was all tensed, Mister Tulane. This was the first time I'd ever matched a gun with another man. Oh, I'd practised with old cans but — "

"You beat him, anyway."

"I never knew how I did it! Mac Heggety had been handling guns for years — and I was just a young feller starting out — not that I ever wanted to be a gun-toter. That man had shot down men before my time — but I beat him to it."

"Maybe you've got swifter reactions than you imagine . . . "

"Maybe. Anyway, I beat him — my slug took him right in the heart. Sheer luck — or was it bad luck? Depends how you figure it. But I got his bullet, too — as you know — in my shoulder."

"Don't start thinking gunplay is the answer to everything," said Wade Tulane. "It ain't. You probably beat him by sheer youthful speed and nervous tension — and maybe Mac Heggety wasn't so fast that day. Being a fast gun isn't exactly a science . . . "

"Thanks for the explanation." Tommy

laughed uncertainly. "Well, I just rode out of that canyon in a scare. I'd seen the man drop and that was pretty grim. I just rode out fast — all thoughts of why the man had been acting so mysteriously forgotten. I rowelled my horse — and then before long I ran into you. As you were a stranger I just kept going because I didn't want to be stopped and answer questions. I guess I acted a bit crazy. Anyway, that was some distance from where Heggety had dropped."

Wade patted the lad's good shoulder. "Tell that account to the sheriff and I reckon he'll accept your story. He's got to — you've got a good character so far. And with so much going on in Laredo, Sheriff Bill Hapner hasn't time to delve into every little ruckus. Let's ride back to town before the sheriff has you on a wanted poster! Anyway, I'm gettin' mighty tired . . . "

"Sure hate to think I was a wanted man," laughed Tommy Camden. "I've written paragraphs about outlaws and always figured there was something to be pitied about a man who is hunted."

Wade stiffened, nodding agreement, his smile vanished. He had almost forgotten he was probably on a wanted list. And now the young man's laughing remark brought the realisation that his time in Laredo could be short. What if there was a wanted poster on the way to the sheriff's office? He might have to ride out, leave Stella and Tommy to their troubles. Leaving the girl behind would be a nasty blow — but that was really illogical because he hardly knew her!

"Let's hit the trail," he said harshly. "Your best plan is to see the sheriff and explain. Don't stay on the dodge. Anyway, let's go before these animals are too tired . . ."

"Maybe I'll need some more gun practice because Rip Heggety will be after me."

"Forget it. You're not a gunny. Just leave him to me. As you and your sister can see — an' anyone else — I've got gunman stamped all over me!" Wade was grimly sarcastic at that point.

"That's mighty fine of you. I guess Stella and me need friends. You think I should ride back and go to Sheriff Hapner? He scared me when he called at the store . . . "

"I say you're going back," said Wade abruptly. "No more talk! Just git going."

But Stella wanted to make a comment. "Wasn't it odd that Tommy should find Mac Heggety in the canyon — as if he was searching for something? There's some mystery there . . . "

"Women's intuition?" muttered Wade. "Wal, maybe. The way I see all this odd business, there's one hombre who knows all the answers — and that's this durned nuisance, Rip Heggety. He could tell you the answers in one damned breath! Why your pa was killed and the drapery store searched — even why they wanted to buy the place." He paused. "Maybe that last question is easy. They wanted to buy the store and house in order to find something — something out of the ordinary. Can't be any other answer."

"But what? There isn't anything of value."

"When they couldn't buy the place legitimately, these guys reckoned to find what they wanted by searching. Wal, maybe we ought to look closely at the store ourselves. And maybe I ought to take a close looksee at that mysterious canyon . . . "

"I'll show you the exact spot," said Tommy. "Unless Bill Hapner sticks me in the jailhouse!"

They started on the long-delayed ride back, and at Tommy's suggestion took a line across country so that they would not cross the tracks of the placer camps and Heggety's potential pals.

They entered Laredo some time later, the night dark and colder, the town seemingly deserted, although some rannigans were still in a saloon, probably on an all-night card-game.

Even the street oil-lanterns had been extinguished, leaving the buildings like black, gaunt shapes. It was an ominous, scary collection of buildings in this collective darkness although in the sunny daylight hours the entire scene could be vastly different. Apart from a huge amount of real business, Laredo had other activities such as meetings in the little adobe church and there had even been a lecturer in the council chamber. The more respectable ranchers regularly met in the Stockman Hotel to talk business and debate the shipment of cattle by the newly-opened railroad, and this kind of association was conducted in a very dignified manner. And many of the neater homes around the town afforded scope for family life and activities.

There was little thought of all this in Wade Tulane's mind as they rode up to the sheriff's office and all three tied their animals to the hitching-rail. There were no other horses in the deserted street.

In the manner of the times, Wade gallantly helped Stella Camden to mount the few steps to the porch, although there was little need. One might have thought she was wearing a bustle instead of the very boyish blue jeans, shirt and buckskin jacket!

On reaching the notice-board outside the office, Wade slowed and gave it a wary glance. Two pictures of wanted men decorated the board but his own face was not there. True, there were few pictures of him to be obtained, but there wasn't an artist's impression either. And even the write-ups of wanted men without pictures did not apply to him — so he began to breathe a bit more easily.

Tommy Camden hammered on a closed door. Maybe the sheriff had retired for the night, a disgruntled man! Maybe he was sleeping in his office. Some lawmen used a big chair as a bed and lived rough. Maybe they wouldn't waken the sheriff.

But then bolts were pulled and Bill

Hapner stood outlined in lamplight in the doorway, a gun in his fist and a glare on his visage. But he wasn't surprised to see his visitors.

"Thought you'd see some sense!" he barked. He rubbed his bristly chin. He was still chewing and swallowing some food — it seemed the sheriff had been consuming a very late supper. They went inside his office, a sheaf of papers on the desk near to the mug of coffee and plate of sandwiches attracting Wade's eyes. More wanted notices!

"I want to tell you exactly what happened out by the desert buttes between Mac Heggety an' me," faltered Tommy.

"Not before time! You could have saved me some trail-pounding!"

Tommy launched out on the same account of events that he had related to Wade, being quite accurate and not glossing over facts for the lawman's benefit. It was just as well he was exact in his narrative for Bill Hapner shot some shrewd questions at him that would have tripped him up had he not been telling the truth. The tale took some time in telling, and as Bill Hapner doggedly ate his sandwiches and rapped questions, Wade felt some pangs of hunger. Gawd, he hadn't eaten a good meal for some time!

At last the sheriff came out with his disgruntled judgement. "You can go, young feller. I'm the law around here — an' there ain't much of it — so you get the benefit of the doubt. I ain't locking you up, if that's what you feared. Guess it was a fair fight an' I'll tell the mayor and the town committee that when we meet. Don't get into more grief with guns. This town is full of hellions. I keep tellin' the mayor that but all he does is hum an' haw!"

"He won't get into any more trouble," drawled Wade. "At least I sure hope not. But I ain't so sure others will accept it this way. I mean that rannigan Rip Heggety won't take your judgement, Sheriff!"

"Git!" snapped the sheriff. "I can't protect every doggone fool in this town. I'll talk to this Rip galoot — ain't no more I can do. Now git — I want some sleep tonight!"

They returned to the animals at the hitching-rail, Wade thinking: "Maybe now I can get some supper." It sure was late, and they were really tired, but he was loath to leave the girl's presence. Maybe she had some good food on hand. Maybe she'd invite him in if he made it obvious he'd like to dally!

It was wishful thinking but oddly it came true. "Why don't you come to our house, Wade?" The invitation was honest and without guile, as Stella smiled at him. "I think we have some cold pie."

"Yeah come in and have a bite," added Tommy. "I don't know how to thank you . . . "

"Don't try . . . "

The house was warm and nicely furnished, with a big armchair covered in chintz which Wade was invited to use. With a plate of beef pie in his hand and a mug of coffee nearby, Wade watched the girl as she moved around the room. She had youthful grace, a litheness of body that held his eyes captive although he tried not to embarrass her by staring. The feeling slowly dawned on him that he was without a decent woman in his life, a kind of maverick. What did he own — call his own? Two guns? God, that was pitiful! and a good horse! But there was more to life, as other men had discovered, than these fool things. A real home was a prized possession — and a family — maybe a son and a daughter to dangle on a knee!

These sudden strange thoughts were madness, he decided, brought on by a warm home, some food and the proximity of a pretty girl. Maybe these comfortable things of life were not for him!

Although he had prolonged the visit, Wade had to leave because the night was getting really late and they were all tired. His horse was at the tie-rail outside the drapery store and house and really needed to be taken to the livery.

"I'll see tomorrow about that ride to the canyon," he announced.

"Sure." Tommy nodded. "If I'm tied to some work maybe Sis can show you the place."

Stella smiled, eyes meeting Wade across the room. Did he see invitation in that gaze — or was he fooling himself. "Of course," she murmured. "I'd be glad to go with you . . . "

Wade nodded and took his leave.

The store door shut behind him with the jangle of the bell that operated when the door moved, and he was about to step forward across the boardwalk to get his horse when an over-anxious voice snarled from across the street:

"I got a bead on you, feller. Say your prayers!"

Wade froze, nerves instantly tight, his eyes searching the dark shadows on the other side — but he could not see any human form. The vengeful voice had snarled from some locked-up buildings, all shrouded in darkness. As the first few seconds of the grim challenge ticked off Wade realised the man did not intend to shoot and get it over with. No — it was a cat-and-mouse game, with the challenger sure of his hand.

Grimly, taut with anger and tiredness, Wade tried to discern the slightest movement in the deep gloom across the way but there was not even a variation of shade on shade. The mystery man was really hidden, with a death slug in his gun. There was absolutely nothing to fire at, not even a suspicion of a solid real man.

With every nerve and muscle tensed, Wade stood on the boardwalk and felt cold things crawl up his spine. He thought Rip Heggety must be somewhere across the street, a menace of a man, an enemy who wanted him dead. Then the voice gloated:

"You are a blasted interferin' skunk!

You have got in my way! I don't like that. Who the hell are you? I'll tell you — a dead man! You beat me up down by the river! I hate having to kill you as easy as this. A slug is too fast, hombre! I'd sooner smash you to pulp bit by bit! You were lucky to beat me in fisticuffs! You couldn't do it again — not to Rip Heggety."

The man was trying to boast.

"Put away your gun an' come out o' there and try me with your fists," Wade invited. "You want satisfaction, huh? Why not try your luck? Or have you really got a yellow streak?"

He was attempting to trick the man on the basis that anything was better than being a motionless target for a bullet!

A snarl greeted the suggestion. "Go to hell! You figure to talk your way out, huh? Start praying, feller. You crossed a real mean guy when you crossed me!"

"Are you so yellow you got to hide!" Wade taunted. "Come on out and give me a chance to draw!"

With cold fear in his guts, Wade hoped for some reaction, but even if the other came forward and into some moonlight to make it a straight fight he wondered if his hands would move fast enough. Wade was sure he was stiff with over-tension.

"Nothing doing!" chuckled the other man. "I'm just going to kill you real dead, mister. Let me tell you something — just so you know I'm a smart hombre — I knew I'd get you comin' out of that house because I saw your hoss at the tie-rail. And after you get your come-uppance I'll fix that young swine, Tommy Camden. I'm tellin' you all this because you won't live to see it. And that flamin' gal! I guess I hate the lot of you!"

Wade dived. Like lightning he figured that no man could spit out even a few hundred words without relaxing a fraction.

Wade dived for the stone water-trough he had noted right from the start of this confrontation. It lay at least six yards away at the edge of the boardwalk, a mecca for thirsty animals usually. Normally, he would have opined that no man could beat a slug fired by an accurate gun and travel six yards at the same time. But the impossible is always achieved by a man in a moment of terrific effort.

He shot for the cover of the stone horse-trough in a tremendous rush that ended in a dive so forceful that he thudded into the trough and felt pain rasp through his shoulder. Simultaneously, Rip Heggety's gun snapped off two spiteful shots that spat through the air in seconds, but they just missed Wade Tulane because of his desperate leap. Then Wade was a huddled man, behind the trough, his hand tugging at his gun. It was clear of leather, ready for action while he gulped for breath. Safe, so far! He'd just missed death! But grimly he did not underestimate his adversary, for the man was in the hellion class all right!

Wade ventured to poke out his gun from behind cover and flung off two shots into the darkness across the narrow street. It was just action to let the other man know he had a fight on his hands. He wanted to edge Rip Heggety out of the deep gloom he had chosen for his hiding-place.

He chanced a glance across the street as his shots plugged the darkness. Then muzzle-flame spat viciously from a certain spot and a slug bit into the earth only inches from his leg. Heggety might be getting the range — or maybe he was lucky. He kept under cover and then sighted on the spot where the orange flame had flashed. He triggered twice again — and then rammed back into the cover of the solid stone horse-trough. He kept his head well down and reloaded.

To his grim disgust there was no cry of pain in answer to his shots. So he had not plugged the devil!

Wade whipped off two more shots

over the top of the trough just in case Heggety was getting an angle on him. The slugs once again tore somewhere into the dark building across the street. Wade shifted position, keeping under cover, and then slipped more shells into his gun.

Suddenly, he heard the sound of an approaching man behind him, from the corner of the alley, down the side of the drapery store. Wade half turned. God, who the hell was this? Then a voice hissed. "It's me — Tommy!"

With relief Wade snapped, "Keep back. It's Rip Heggety across the street."

"I want to help you kill him . . . "

"Keep outa this!" snapped Wade tensely. "It's not in your league. Don't be a fool."

"I've gotta help . . . "

There were no more words for a rataplan of shots bit all around the stone horse-trough and chips of rock dug at Wade and he involuntarily closed his eyes. He waited. All those shots meant that the other man had emptied his gun.

Three seconds after the last slug dug viciously into the stone trough, Wade Tulane launched out on another jet-propelled dive — this time across the width of the street. He shot over so fast that showers of grit spurted from his boots. His gun blazed at every yard he covered. It was a form of cover but he did not let himself slow down. Speed was invaluable.

He reached the side of the building which was opposite to the drapery store, which meant he was on the same side of the street as the gunman. He flattened while he dragged in some rasping breath and used the moments to reload his gun. Strangely, he thought this rumpus was certainly eating the shells. Now to trick Rip Heggety . . .

Wade took off his hat and slid it gingerly around the corner of the building which gave him cover. It was an old trick but it brought a response. Two more shots tore through the night air and the hat whisked away. Good shooting from the enemy!

Wade did not spend any time regretting the holes that would be in his hat. Maybe Stella had some new ones in their store! He slid back along the clapboard wall of the building and sidled around the rear of the place. Maybe he could take the other guy from behind. However, he did not underestimate the villain and already the man might realise that he could be circled.

Wade was inching along the back of the high square building when there came an enraged bellow from somewhere down the street.

"Drop your hoglegs, you durned hellions, an' quit fouling this town! This is the sheriff!"

Wade grinned thinly. Sheriff Bill Hapner had emerged to investigate the shooting but it would take more than words and the mention of the law to deter the thick-headed Rip Heggety. This cuss was now blind to all reason.

The next corner of the wood building was reached, allowing Wade to pause and consider, but then he chanced the look he just had to take.

It was a quick darting movement of his head, no more, and then back to cover. During that second he got a glimpse of the alley and figured it was empty, filled only by the pervading darkness. He thought grimly that he was a shadow playing a dangerous game among other shadows.

With this precarious trust in his instinct, he slid around into the darkness of the alley, his gun preceding him. He got around the sharp corner of the building and continued to sidle like a ghost. His boots hunted into the dust, silent, like a padding animal. It seemed that Rip Heggety was still hidden in the gloom made by the overhanging porch at the front. Not by a single sound in the night must he suspect that he was being hunted.

Another angry bawl shouted through the thin night air.

"Get out o' that, you ornery jaspers! I want law and order in the streets! Hit the trail!"

It seemed maybe the sheriff did not realise who was engaged in the gunplay and maybe distinctions did not matter to the lawman when he heard gunshots. All disturbers of the peace were poison to him!

Reaching the next corner of the building, Wade had to halt because this was a danger point. When he slid around this edge it would have to be with his gun blazing inside a shattered second!

Not unnaturally he had to nerve himself. For a crazy fleeting moment he wondered why he was risking death because of some homicidal gunny when he could be minding his own business, and then he decided he'd got into this set-up of his own volition and it was his job to settle it. But he was just a man and his courage could ebb or strengthen as circumstances allowed. Then in another grim second a sombre mood possessed him and gave him the impetus he needed.

A picture of Stella Camden flashed strangely into the camera of his brain, illustrating the danger to the girl, something he knew he had to dispose of. He would do what was needed, thinking of her and her femininity.

And he was forming a hatred of Rip Heggety. That was almost enough.

He slid around the sharp corner, his gun poking a way through the thin night air.

6

Leo Sands's Offer

WADE saw the other man instantly.

Rip Heggety was in a doorway, the shadows enfolding him almost completely, and from the other side of the roadway he was just part of the blackness. But now, on the same side as this menacing individual, Wade could see him clear enough. Looking down the side of the clapboard wall, Wade could see the man's dark shape as an entity, as varying shade against the black night that had served him so well.

Grimly, feeling like a killer, he triggered, his gun requiring no levelling.

Even as he shot, everything was confusion, actions contained in split seconds. Rip Heggety had sensed his presence and wheeled, his gun blazing slugs and flame. Wade had fired, too — so swiftly he hardly realised how many times he triggered. Orange flame lanced the gloom. Slugs should have beaten any possible human reaction.

Wade heard the guns roar but he never had the chance to smell the gunsmoke. With the vengeful bark of guns he felt an agonising, searing pain in his head. Something red-hot burned his skull like a poker taken from a fire. Blinding lights shot through his vision and then there was darkness which was different to the night air.

He did not know that he fell as the darkness possessed his brain. In fact, Wade Tulane knew nothing as he thudded backwards to the hard ground.

As to Rip Heggety, he had the luck of his species. He had jerked when he saw Wade at the corner, gun spitting redly, and the man triggered frantically, slouching into the gunman's position almost with one movement. Seconds saved him.

He knew it was time to back out of this rumpus, an impulse which he put into effect. He rammed against the locked door behind him, in the alcove which had sheltered him, with bull-like strength, and the door gave and he fell into the space beyond. He was clear, out of the trap. Moments later he wrenched at a door at the side of the building — and then he was out into the night. Boots crunched noisily and quickly into grit as he made his getaway. He was going for his hidden horse.

He was sure that his enemy had been hit in the fusillade. No shots sought his position; no gun tracked him as he went off.

He figured he had hit the other galoot. Hopefully, the interfering swine was dead!

Wade wasn't able to hear the rapid thud of hoofs as the man rode off. Wade could not hear anything, nor see the way people collected swiftly in the street even at that late hour. He did not know that Stella Camden was the first to reach him, her eyes bright with fear and a choking cry in her throat. Then there were others on the scene, helping hands that lifted him and carried him indoors.

A long time later he opened his eyes to stare uncomprehendingly at the girl, painfully at first because his head ached and felt full of shooting-stars. With heavy eyes he looked into her face, unable to think.

"Where am I?" The muttered remark was simply a sign that he was still alive.

"In Miss Stella's bedroom!" barked a voice. The sheriff was angry, sick and tired of gunnies. "You got a nice crease down your cranium, Mister Tulane. Another half-inch and you'd be a candidate for Boot Hill!"

"Now don't bother him, Sheriff," pleaded the girl.

"Aw, he's a hardcase," growled the sheriff.

"I wish the doctor was here,"

exclaimed the girl. "But as you say, he's out at the Bar M on a childbirth case."

"That galoot will get over this," snapped the sheriff. "Wal, he's in good hands, I reckon, if you're carin' for him, Miss Stella. Should think himself lucky . . . reckon he's one of these hardy types who can stand being thrown over a cliff . . . I'd say he'll be wanting the hide of Heggety as soon as he can swing his feet off this bed."

"Heggety! Murderous ruffian!" Tommy Camden looked full of fury now that he had allied himself with Wade. He was holding strips of cloth which he had torn into bandages. "He laid an ambush for Wade — right outside our house! I don't know what happened exactly . . . first thing I knew I was hearing shots . . . then I went out of the back to see what it was all about . . . "

"Good thing you had the savvy to use the back of your house and not the front," snapped the sheriff dryly.

Tommy swung to him. "What do you figure to do about this, Bill Hapner?"

The sheriff's moustache twitched as he returned angrily: "Nothing! I can't stop fools throwing lead at each other. I can't stop fair fights! It seems to be part of our times — but it ain't law and order and I look forward to the day when a town can be a peaceful place and somethin' to be proud of. The way this darned town is going, it's almost too much for one man and two deputies. So we've got a lawless town. Will it ever be any better? If Tulane here kills Heggety in a fair fight it ain't goin' to worry me none. But if either jasper commits murder then by heck it's my duty to see he gets a trial and a hang-noose party!"

And with that statement of his philosophy, for what it was worth, the sheriff of Laredo stamped angrily out of the room.

When Tommy and Stella looked back at Wade, he had swung his legs down to the floor. He sat and fought swimming sensations in his brain, conscious of the blood at the side of his head. Touching the wound, he discovered a painful bruise along his temple. Stella turned to him. "Oh, you can't move yet! You mustn't!"

"I've got to get on my feet." He tried to smile. "I've still got my boots on! Aw, heck, that's not much of a joke! Anyway, I'm alive, huh! So I didn't get Rip Heggety?"

"He got away, Wade — he had a horse somewhere."

"Yeah, his sort always have. Wal, he didn't salivate me, huh?" Wade's attempted grin brought pains to his head.

"You really need Doc Thorne," said the girl. "But he's out of town and at this hour of the night we'll just have to make do. I've cleaned the side of your head — maybe you need a bandage fixing there."

"So he nearly got me," admitted Wade.

The girl nodded, her concerned eyes

meeting his, and Wade saw something there that no other woman had shown him.

She was very firm with him and he had to submit to having the bandage wound around his head. He wouldn't lie back, no matter how much she insisted. After his first few glances around the room, he realised it was Stella's room by the feminine touches. Nice drapes and a vase of flowers met his inquiring gaze. A dress with tacking stitches lay at the side of a sewing-machine and there was a faint perfume in the air. Wade felt vaguely embarrassed, unused to femininity. He actually got off the bed and stood up. It was an effort but he made it. He was conscious that his dusty clothes, heavy boots and thick shirt were strangely out of place in this girl's room. He had a feeling, in spite of his ablutions earlier in the day at the hotel, that he still smelled of horse!

"Guess I'd better go," he muttered with a strange, shy grin. "This ain't the

DT10

place for me, Miss Stella. Maybe I'm more suited to a hideout in the ground! I'm going . . . maybe I won't walk into gun-grief again. See you tomorrow about that ride to the canyon."

His black horse had been tied to the rail all during the shooting rumpus and the animal had calmed by the time he reached it. The horse snorted a welcome as he touched its black hide and he spent some minutes fondling the crittur's neck. "I ain't lookin' after you very well, hoss," he muttered. "Wal, I'll change all that in a few moments, huh?"

He unhitched the animal and swung slowly to the saddle and rode back to the livery along the main drag. He left the horse, taking off the leathers and the saddle because the old horse-wrangler who ran the livery was asleep in a corner away from the other animals left for the night. The wrangler would no doubt rub down the black in the morning and feed and water him.

Wade walked wearily back to the

Bonanza Hotel, nodded to a bald-headed guy drinking whisky at the reception desk and then proceeded to his room. He noticed about three late-night drinkers in the saloon, playing poker probably, because that was a game that hooked the participants and could go on all night. The men meant nothing to him — no identification either way.

In his room he locked the door and lighted the lamp. He went to the window and saw there was a sheer drop to the yard below, so he left the window half-open. Although the night brought comparative coolness to these parts, the air in the room seemed warm and sluggish.

He knew the slug crease had stopped any thought he might entertain about pursuing his attacker. He wasn't up to it. Weariness could be dangerous, so any further tangle with Rip Heggety would have to wait. Somehow he didn't doubt that there was further antagonistic action to come.

He dropped off his boots, thinking oddly of Stella Camden and her concern for him. A lovely girl — but was he the right man for her? Shaking his head, he took off his belts and hung them on the brass rail at the head of the bed. He felt the bandage around his cranium and decided the bleeding had stopped. It was an odd thought — but he could be a cadaver right now in which case there'd be no enmity, no strife — and no thoughts about a pretty girl!

He considered undressing and then, trail habit being strong, decided against. He flipped back the top blanket and lay on the bed, pulling the covering back over his body — and then a crazy thought — this way of living would have to stop if he had a woman like Stella Camden to keep him company at nights!

It was a mad thought. His head sank to the pillow and he fell into sound sleep. He would lie like that until sun-up, or until something interrupted his rest. Something? Something like an intruder, he reckoned . . . and he'd know even if sound asleep.

It was as well for Wade Tulane's peace of mind that he did not see Leo Sands ride out of town early that morning when news of the shooting had spread around. Leo Sands took the trail down to the River Shasta, the sun-filled morn making his progress easy. With a head full of vengeful thoughts, he wasted little time appreciating the cloudless sky, the baying of cattle in a distant grassy valley. The determined way he rode his well-behaved pony showed he had made up his mind about some course of action.

He rode into the placer camp some time later, a dandified figure in a black coat and new hat, and halted to ask a question of a man at the nearest tent.

"Rip Heggety? Yep. He's got a claim down by them willows, turn of the river — you'll see 'em." The man paused. "But what the hell do you want with a hellion like that?"

"My business, amigo." Leo Sands rode on, satisfied he'd locate the man he wanted. There might be some delay, this part of the terrain sprawled for some miles; the river was now low and the gold-miners panning for dust cursing the lack of moving water because those currents brought down the dust from the hills.

Leo Sands knew that Rip Heggety had tried to kill Wade Tulane, the interfering guy from out of town. The news was all over the saloons from the first moment the doors opened that morn. Even the story of how Tulane had beat up Heggety down by the river had got around, probably by some visiting miner that night. Most men of the hardened type knew now that Heggety sought revenge.

Leo Sands had seen Wade return to the Bonanza Hotel, his head bandaged, and he guessed he had visited Stella Camden, a fact that soured him. The interfering rannigan had just too much luck! Somebody should stop his run of good fortune!

When Leo Sands finally located the placer claim by the willows he did, in fact, find Rip Heggety there, which was his luck because the hellion could have been anywhere. The young miner rose from his smouldering camp-fire and stood with one hand on a gun-butt, his feet planted apart, sullen truculence all over his face. He was dirty with river muck, unshaven and suspicious.

"What the hell do you want?"

"You know me . . . "

"Yeah — gambling-man, eh. I've seen you play . . . you make dinero the easy way, feller . . . "

"Maybe some day I could put you in the way of a winning streak, huh, amigo? You know — fix the cards — with some mug!"

"Say your piece. You ain't come all this way just for that crap."

Leo Sands dismounted and carelessly flung his pony's leathers over a willow branch, coming forward, his white face smiling.

"Let's talk, Heggety. I've heard you've tangled bad with Tulane, that son-of-a-bitch stranger. You know he's still alive?"

"Yeah — I guessed. What's it to you?" Anger still decorated Heggety's grim features.

"I'd like you to kill the swine . . . " muttered Leo Sands. He brought out a pack of the new-type factory-made cigarettes and offered them to the other man. Rip Heggety took the brown-paper cylinder, examined it suspiciously and then picked up a reddened bit of wood from the fire. Both men lit up.

"So I wish the hardcase dead!" sneered Heggety. "And if he crosses my trail he will be a cadaver this time! Ain't he the lucky one! I don't stand for any man beating me up." He glared again at Leo Sands. "He bashed my goddam head against a rock! Why, I've a good mind to ride back right now and blast him where I find him!"

"He's in bed. And he's got friends in town — including the sheriff — "

"And that gal, I hear," sneered Rip Heggety. "Don't that put you out? I hear you was aimin' high with that gal!"

"We'll get him." Leo Sands spoke with soft enmity.

"What's your complaint?"

"He crossed me. I was in a fight with a gink called Latimer and Tulane shot the gun out of my hand. Near blamed took my fingers away — and me a gambler — my hand!"

"Ornery cuss, ain't he?" sneered Rip Heggety. He dragged on the cigarette, consuming half of it savagely. "He just hits town and starts raising hell all around. But I'll git him. I'll git him just when I'm right an' ready. He's had too much luck. I'll even with that young pig Tommy Camden, too. I'll teach him to kill my brother. He killed Mac . . . "

"I know about that. The news got around. And — get this, Heggety — it looks like the sheriff lapped up that young swine's yarn because he's back home. The sheriff didn't put him in jail for killing your brother."

Rip Heggety boasted savagely: "I'm adding him to my list, but before he's dead there's somethin' I want from him. Something I got to settle with that young cuss . . . "

"You could clean up all round — a galoot like you," encouraged Leo Sands. "Fix Tulane good and dead — and that young cuss Tommy Camden. I don't know what it is you want from young Camden — I don't get that — but I want to have the girl — Stella — "

"Heck — wimmen," sneered Heggety. "That your angle? Hey — the saloons are full of them."

"Not like that girl . . . she's special . . . the kind I want . . . "

"Now I've heard everything," sneered Heggety. "You want a woman — take her!"

"I don't give a damn for your

opinion." Leo Sands reddened angrily. "I want Stella Camden. I wanted to marry her. She damned turned me down — me, a gentleman. Yessir!" His flush vanished and the pallor returned to his cheeks. "Turned me down — the whole goddam town knows that! I can't take that. You get that stupid brother of hers out of the way and that Tulane hombre — and I'll be mighty glad."

"That all? You want me to do your dirty work? Gun work, huh? Are you yellow? Go git him yourself!"

"I'll pay you."

"The hell you will. I got a placer here that pays off — when I get around to workin' on it — and I got ideas for more dinero — big, big money — when Tommy Camden gets around to talking to me about a certain subject. Anyway, to hell with you, mister. I don't want your silver dollars — gold is more my line."

"I'll help you get Tulane and Tommy Camden — at a later date," snapped

Leo Sands. "I could be useful . . . maybe a tip-off . . . something . . . "

"You're not being smart. I'll get those two without your help — when I'm ready — especially Camden. He killed my brother . . . "

"Just figured on being sure. Good to know your friends, huh?"

"And enemies . . . "

"Just wanted to let you know you can count on me," added Leo Sands.

Rip Heggety turned sullenly to the fire and kicked the embers. "I got pals already — good ones. Hey, Dutch — come outa that tent. We got company. Show your face."

Rip had to go into the tent and shake the man who was inside. When he emerged again, there was a big bearded miner with him, a character who seemed to be plastered with river mud. His trousers and shirt were caked and the muck was on his beard. He had a leathery round face and narrow eyes that no man in his right senses would trust.

"Here's a feller who knows how to stack the cards, Dutch. So don't play with him or maybe he'll take that damned cache from you!" And Rip Heggety laughed recklessly as he made the crude introduction.

"Don' wan' to gamble witt anyones right now," mumbled the man. His strange accent slowed his speech. "Iss keepin' gold — ya. Dere will be time when Dutch big rich mans."

"My pard," sneered Rip Heggety. "He does all the rough graft. He'll fight anytime I ask — with fists. But he's not much with guns. Don't know that I need your help, Sands."

"You might. All right, I've had my say — long damned ride — but forget that. You know how I feel. Just one more thing. Is it correct you and your brother killed William Camden those few weeks back?"

"What's it to you? You get plumb to hell outa here, mister. I ain't saying no and I ain't saying yeah." His laughter increased to a bellow as if he considered there was something very funny in that subject.

Leo Sands turned to his pony. “All right! I don’t give a damn. Soon as that girl is alone, she’ll be right glad to have me around. Remember that, Heggety — that’s what I want.”

The air was full of bawling laughter as Dutch joined his partner in merriment. Dutch had a voice fit to waken the dead spirits in the distant City of Ghosts, an old labyrinth of caves and homes carved out of solid rock by an age-old tribe of forgotten Indians and now a home for bats and coyotes outside Laredo.

Leo Sands had to ride away. The visit had been a bit of a failure, he grudgingly admitted, but he had shown Rip Heggety that he sided with him. And yet he had only contempt for a thick-head like the Heggety man because brains with that tough seemed to be lacking. Maybe something might come of the situation . . .

He rode away from the placer mines,

conscious that he had said enough. And he meant everything he had said about the girl — because she was beginning to be an obsession. When he got her — and he would — he'd teach her a lesson in humility, show her that he was a real man and to be taken seriously.

Musing during the ride, he did not doubt that the Heggety brothers had killed William Camden, although the reason for this seemed shrouded in mystery. One of the Heggety men was dead and Rip would surely get Tommy Camden for that act. And maybe the same hellion would get revenge when Wade Tulane hit the dust. Maybe Rip Heggety would act soon, but if he went into town he might encounter the sheriff or a deputy. Maybe Rip Heggety would want to fight it out in gunsmoke, spurning a cold-blooded but easier murder. These tough in-bitten men had that much pride in the power of the gun.

Leo Sands sneered inwardly at the stupidity of these ideas. He urged his pony on, along the easy trail back to town, an environment that was really home to him. Damn these trails!

There was maybe time for a few hands of cards in one of the saloons where a real mug could be found and some easy money picked up. Yeah — back to business — for the time being!

7

Burning Bullets

WADE TULANE felt a lot better the next morning as he examined the slug crease at the side of his head. The hot bullet had taken skin and hair away, which might leave a scar. He smiled faintly into the mirror as he considered that this was better than a one-way trip to Boot Hill.

He ran over the whole set-up, mentally. Rip Heggety wanted him dead. And Heggety would like Tommy Camden on the end of a Colt as vengeance for the death of his ruffian brother! That was the basis for the hatred — but there was something else. Something behind the killing of William Camden, draper, who never harmed anyone. Why should the Heggety brothers kill a mere draper? Why should they attempt to force the sale of the shop?

With these thoughts in mind, Wade remembered he had practically promised to ride out to the canyon where William Camden had been found dead.

He breakfasted at the Bonanza Hotel on good grub, bacon and beans — better than trail-cooking, anyway. Then he called at Stella's drapery emporium, the first customer that morning. He grinned, stupidly shy as the girl came forward to greet him.

"Would you like to come into the living-room," she began but he held up a hand.

"I'm a customer . . . "

"You?"

"Yeah. I want to buy a hat," he said gravely. "I lost mine last night — and anyway I guess it has a hole in it."

"I thought most range-riders were proud of their old hats . . . "

"I see you have some Stetsons and sombreros . . . "

"Help yourself. I won't take payment. You've helped us."

"That ain't no way to run a business." He grinned. He stared across the counter at a pile of thick shirts favoured by riders. "Maybe I ought to buy me a new shirt! Yep — and I guess a man can always do with new socks."

Just balking to this delightful girl was all the excuse he wanted. He felt he'd buy anything she wanted to sell!

She laughed, conscious of his masculinity, noting he was freshly shaved and smelled nicely of carbolic soap. She brought out three Stetsons, which were telescoped into each other. Sorting them out she placed them on the counter, her flushed cheeks betraying the excitement she felt in just talking to him. "I think you'd better try one, Wade — unless you're just trying to drum up trade for me!"

"Nope. I really need a new hat and a shirt an' a pair o' socks." He tried on a fawn Stetson and glared critically across at a mirror. "Got a nice brim — guess it will keep the sun out of my eyes . . . " He paused. "Is Tommy away at his job?"

"Yes. He had to go out."

"Howsabout that ride to the canyon? I'd sure like to ride that way with you . . . Don't know why I want to see the place — just some queer hunch — 'cos Tommy's account of how Mac Heggety was riding through seems a bit odd."

"Tommy told me to say that if you went over to the Laredo Journal office he'd get the time off."

"It would be great if you could ride with me."

"Oh, I wish I could, Wade, but I've got customers who think the store should be open most of the time. Anyway, I'd like to thank you for — for — everything."

"Somehow I don't think it's over," he said grimly. He handed over the money to pay for his goods. "I want you to know I think it's a favour to be helping you, Stella."

He had to leave the store, reluctantly, because there was a simple pleasure in just being near this lovely creature, but there was work to do. He stuck his new hat on. He did not use the new shirt. It would only gather dust and sweat if he was going to ride to the canyon.

He went on to the livery where the black was rested and fed. He handed out some more cash to the old wrangler — who didn't seem as fresh as the horse — as he slipped on the headstall and fastened the saddle and cinch. The black rubbed a velvety nose against him. Then Wade rode out. "Adios, wrangler!"

Wade found Tommy Camden at the small wood building which served as a printing-works and office for the Laredo Journal. As Wade entered the printing-room, an elderly man wearing a green apron glanced up. Wade concluded this was Ben Smith, the boss Tommy had mentioned.

The young brother of Stella Camden came out of a tiny cubby-hole of an office upon hearing the sound of Wade's entrance and soon introductory remarks were made.

"William Camden was a friend of mine," said Ben Smith. "And I'd like his killer brought to justice — and if there was more than one that goes for them all. I stand with the sheriff for law and order, needed if this town is to progress. One day Laredo will be an important centre for everything that creates wealth and jobs. Yessir, the most important place in Texas! And we aim to grow with it . . . " Conscious that he was sounding like a politician, and that Wade was smiling, the old man broke off. "Tommy has told me how you've helped him so far."

"Maybe he can get time off to ride with me this morn," suggested Wade.

"Sure, if it's important. He hasn't got regular hours here, anyway."

The conversation concluded, Tommy went back to the stable behind their drapery store and saddled his horse. Wearing shirt and brown cords for the ride, he rejoined Wade and some minutes later the two men rode out of town with a clatter of hoofs as they allowed the animals to skim off their freshness.

The trip to the canyon where William Camden had been bushwacked was about twelve miles out into semi-desert country where tufts of hardy grasses grew in well-spaced clumps. They were many miles to the eastern side of the River Shasta, where the beneficial effects of water had long disappeared. There were flowers tucked under the creosote bushes; the inevitable clumps of sage sent up a powerful aroma when disturbed by the horses. Cacti blossomed with spiked points and vivid red flowers. This dryland was studded with saguaro cacti, ironwood and catclaw clumps that tore at riders who got too close. On the ground they frequently saw the queer S-curved tracks of sidewinders. Buzzards and hawks frequented the many valleys, soaring slowly against a blue sky. The sun was a yellow orb that soon had the horses and men sweating.

Eventually the two riders entered the canyon, Tommy pointing silently, mouth dry and words difficult. The walls rose sheer and fairly tall, formed of yellow sandstone scoured into strange shapes and markings by the winds and rains of hundreds of winters. The canyon bed was flat yellow sand, studded with boulders that had lain undisturbed for hundreds of years, and the gullies held the inevitable cholla cactus. Half-way down the silent place Tommy reined in his horse and pointed to the wall on his left.

"That's where I found Mac Heggety — snooping around — peering at this and that."

Wade stared. "It's just a durned canyon. Like a lot more. But you say Heggety was examining the canyon wall?"

"He was. As if he was searching for somethin'. Just staring and examining the walls — though what the heck he expected to find has me beat."

"Show me where your pa was found dead."

Silently, the young man urged his horse forward, very slowly, down the canyon. When he stopped the animal's movement, he was very close to the canyon wall. "About here, Wade. So far as I know, of course, because two ranchers riding this way looking for lost calves found him and brought him back to town only a few hours after he'd been killed."

"That was pure chance, huh? Might have lain here for days or weeks afore anyone came thisaway. I have a feeling this canyon is a strange place — first your pa, and then you shot Mac Heggety." Wade stared up at the yellow sandstone walls, noting the grooves scoured by winds and rains during the years.

"Sure have to admit it's queer that Mac Heggety should ride this way. If he and his brother killed your pa, why should Mac want to ride thisaway again and look like he had lost something? You figure those two bad-hats dropped something around here?"

"I don't think so. I've got a hunch it's something weirdly different. Remember they tried to bulldoze us into selling the store a bit later — and then they ransacked the place when it was obvious we wouldn't sell no matter how high the price."

"They were after something — we've agreed on that. Now I figure Rip Heggety will keep on the same trail . . ."

"He'd like us dead. You for crossing him, and me for killing his damned brother."

"I've got a feeling," muttered Wade thoughtfully, "that he won't go gunning for you until he finds that something he and his brother were looking for. Can't say that he'll show me the same consideration!" Wade kept on staring at the canyon wall just above his head. "Say, do I see some queer markings up there or am I getting a bit confused? Maybe they are just wind scourings . . . ”

Tommy stared up for some minutes, undecided. Then he climbed up on his saddle and stood on the leather, to get a better view.

“Just as I thought. Looks like Indian markings on that part of the wall but they’ve been distorted by sand-ladened winds over the centuries. Nothing unusual around here. Why, just a mile past this part of the canyon you can see the City of Ghosts.”

“What the devil is that?”

“The City of Ghosts was given that name a long time ago, I guess by the first westerners who came this way. It’s mostly a lot of old caves which were inhabited by the Indians hundreds of years ago. Different from the Indians today. The cave-dwellers weren’t nomadic. These redskins carved homes in the rock face and must have lived here permanently. They weren’t hunters — at least not all the time. All you can see now are these weather-beaten caves and remains of rock carvings — pretty much like the marks on this part of the canyon wall."

Wade nodded. "I've seen this kinda thing in other territories. I think Mac Heggety was examining these carvings and marks when he saw you."

Tommy climbed down from his saddle. "Sure seems that way . . . "

"And he came gunning for you — and you shot him in self-defence. Which ties up that business."

Tommy turned to Wade, a determined look on his young face. He sat straight in the saddle, a slim lad, wearing his cords, red shirt and black hat. He had a gun in the new holster. There was still a bandage under the shirt but the healing wound was apparently not too painful. "You think Mac Heggety was simply looking at Indian carvings? You don't think he was here because my pa had died here?"

Wade frowned. "It seems the two facts are maybe tied together. Was your pa ever interested in these Injun markings — as a subject — or in the old caves in the City of Ghosts?"

Tommy shook his head. "Can't rightly say he was. Nope. These old remains of lost Indian civilisations was only passing interest. Pa was more interested in community work in town and the church."

Wade turned his horse and glanced along the canyon wall. "How about having a fast pasear to this City of Ghosts? You say it ain't more than a mile or so from here?"

"That's right — but what good will that do?"

Wade grinned back. "Don't rightly know, son. Just figure to take a look at those caves like we're taking a look at these canyon walls. No more importance than that — at the moment — but it's damned obvious there's a mystery somewhere . . . "

Tommy grinned boyishly. "And you're a curious galoot, Wade. Okay — we'll go look at the City of Ghosts."

At that moment the silence of the yellow canyon was shattered by the vicious spang of a bullet.

Wade Tulane felt the deadly missile whistle past his head like an angry hornet. His horse jibbed in a startled way and Tommy instinctively ducked, and then the two animals sprang into full lope, not only spooked by the intended drygulch bullet but impelled on by the abrupt application of spur rowels!

A second later, as they sat jerking horseback, another shot spat close by them. Once again the slug missed Wade by inches as he crouched low against his black.

"It's me that damned gunny is after!" he snarled.

The drygulcher had triggered two near-misses, which was tough luck for him because the two frightened horses were taking their riders out of range at a terrific lick.

A man did not need to be a genius to realise who the enemies were. Rip

Heggety — and maybe a pal. But only one rifle had spat shots so far. Heggety — damn him! So the man had tailed them to the canyon. This place of yellow sandstone and mysteries had already seen two deaths recently. Seemed that Heggety figured on adding a third.

The marksman had shot from the top of the canyonwall, over on the right. He'd used a rifle, probably a Winchester, for that distance, and Wade had noticed the two shots had been trained on him — not Tommy. Maybe that meant something. Did Heggety really want Tommy Camden dead at this moment in time? Eventually, of course, but right now? It was an intriguing thought.

The thud of hoofs on the canyon bed lasted only for some minutes and definitely put some distance between the two grim riders and the would-be assassin. Wade eventually urged his mount into the shelter of a huddle of big boulders. These lay at the end of the canyon, where the walls had partly crumbled into scattered rocks and lay on the flat amid cholla cactus.

Tommy jigged his horse into the same shelter. He calmed his agitated horse while Wade dismounted and hitched his horse's ribbons to a spur of rock.

"No call to allow that gent to use us for fancy shooting and get away with it." Wade looked at his new hat. "Damned near plugged my headgear!"

Grimly replacing the hat, he slid out a Colt; he was wearing only one gun at the moment and not the fancy twin Colts which had attracted so much attention. He began to climb the pile-up of boulders which led to the top of the canyon wall. He slid forward on his stomach when he reached the top part of the high ground. He stared across the downward space of the canyon and tried to find some sign of the other gunman. Maybe a glint of sun on metal might be a giveaway.

For a long time there was nothing

unusual about the arid scene, with silence brooding over the terrain as it had done for hundreds of years. Nothing moved that Wade could pinpoint — unless there was a sidewinder below — and he didn't mean a human one! Then Wade's good eyesight saw the figure of a man moving cautiously through rocky clefts at the top of the canyon wall. Momentarily, the diminutive shape of a man showed — and then he scrambled out of sight.

The range was too far for a Colt slug to traverse. Better to scout around. Probably the man was leaving his vantage-point now that his initial attempt to kill had failed. Maybe he was going for his mount or just taking fresh cover. Wade scrambled down to Tommy Camden. "That would-be murderer is on the other side of this canyon and I think he's going for his cayuse. If we dash over now, he can't see us crossing the flat-bed around here because he's handling his horse."

"Let's go — on foot," said the young

lad eagerly. "We can get among the rocks where the animals can't go and maybe give him a hot time!"

"Don't you be so hot-pants for gunsmoke," warned Wade. "This ain't funny. That guy wants us dead — you know — something to bury! All the same, he can't have this game all his own way."

The invitation to hunt the man seemed to delight Tommy, and he went off with Wade at a fast sprint across the flat sand, avoiding the scattered rocks. Then they hit the first pile-up of boulders and, guns in hand, began slithering through the rocks, using the little gullies between boulders. Soon they were high on the canyon wall, making a way from cover to cover and wary of the unknown killer. Wade led the approach, mostly because he was well-versed in the tricks of lawless hombres. He had a momentary thought that Stella would be angry with him if he led her young brother into a deadly slug.

Wade Tulane knew they could be moving into grief for it was not possible to ascertain where the tricky would-be killer was at any stage. But this was a chance they had to take. Once more he wondered fleetingly about the wisdom of taking an inexperienced young man like Tommy on this kill-or-be-killed expedition! And himself? Why didn't he just get to hell out of it?

There were few answers to these thoughts.

As he was moving ahead of Tommy, he suddenly glimpsed Rip Heggety. Wade looked down from the shelter of a crevice and saw the man below him, busy unhitching a roan that had been hidden in a nook between some rocks.

Unfortunately, Heggety heard or sensed movement above him almost at the same time. He dived for cover like some startled animal — which was just about his description.

So Wade's fast-spitting Colt slug bit into rock just inches above the man.

With the luck of his kind, the in-bitten guy had found cover just a second to the good.

The crack of the gun spooked the roan and with legs kicking like a bronc the animal ran down the narrow defile among the rocks. The narrow slot twisted so abruptly that the horse was out of sight in seconds.

Then a gun spat vengeance from out of the rocks and the slug hissed at Wade but missed him. He heard the clatter of boots on rock, heard the slither of loose shale, and knew that Heggety was moving away. Wade shot a bitter glance from out of cover in the hope that he'd see the other man as a target, but no sign. The sound of boots again assailed his ears as they rasped frantically on rock and chippings, but there was no visible view of the other man. He was moving dexterously through the slots among the pile-up of boulders.

Wade chanced another shot at the huddle of rocks below him and then, grimly, hating this guy, he moved to another vantage-point, hoping to sight the fellow. But it was not to be. The crafty devil was still moving in the cover of the crevices between the rocks. In some places he was evidently squirming through like a rattler in fear. He kept his head down, rule number one! In fact, there was no view of him, even when Wade shifted position once more.

And then, suddenly, a change in tempo and sounds. Wade heard hoofbeats and knew that Heggety had got to his horse and was moving off. The clatter of hoofs lasted only seconds. Wade leaped up, got to a vantage-point of rock and snapped off shots at random, taking pot-luck. Heggety was rowelling his mount through a narrow slot in the pile of rocks, pushing through catclaw that almost choked the slot and would undoubtedly give rider and horse some bad scratches. Then, as the shots stopped because Wade needed to reload, the man turned the horse around another twist in the defile and was lost to view.

"Damn the feller!" Wade was furious with the result; totally angry with this gunplay. If he had to kill a man, he would wish to get it over as soon as possible.

But not this time, apparently!

8

Successful Search

MAKING him more angry than ever, the next view of Heggety was as a distant figure on a tearing horse. Man and animal were plunging over the barren ground at the entrance to the canyon. Wade stared, mouthing curses, then he turned and tapped Tommy Camden on the arm. "C'mon — let's fork the horses. We've lost the swine an' wasted some shells."

They scrambled down the chaotic masses of broken rock and boulders to the canyon floor and then raced across, but by the time they got to their horses it was obvious Rip Heggety had crossed the flatland and was now tearing through the broken terrain beyond.

Wade and the young fellow sent the horses in a mad chase across the arid land and then pulled up, undecided, as they encountered numerous gullies. The fleeing man could have taken any one.

"Looks like he lights out mighty fast when things don't go his way!" snapped Wade Tulane. "You know somethin' — I'm damned sick and tired of this guy. Now if he was dead, we'd have no more grief! Aw, hell! I shouldn't have to think like this!"

"You could pack it in . . . "

"No — damnation!"

"He must have been trailing us again," commented Tommy. "Maybe he saw us leave town . . . that man's determination to see us dead gives me the shudders!"

"Me more than you," corrected Wade. "It was me he sighted his shells on. Confirms my hunch that he ain't gonna kill you, young feller, until he gets what he was looking for at your store!"

"Great — better not talk to Stella like this."

"She won't like all this damned manhunt stuff . . . "

"We haven't anything of interest to Heggety at our store or the house," commented the young guy.

"Must be something. Why were the Heggety boyos so keen to buy you out . . . "

"Yeah — but I can't think of anything. The idea of Mac or Rip Heggety taking an interest in draperies is a bit ludicrous." Tommy shook his head. "Wade, that jasper has rode off but he'll try again. It's — it's — like some damned vendetta! I feel I've dragged you into this . . . "

"I got myself in when I met Stella." Wade grinned that shy look that changed his stern face. "Heck, I maybe shouldn't say that to you — her brother! And I've tangled with Heggety on my own account, so — "

Momentarily, he thought of the events up in Colorado and wondered if the law up there wanted him, or had the killing of Jack Rawkin been forgotten? But that was another issue.

They continued the ride to the City of Ghosts, stopping only to allow the horses to nuzzle into some water poured into a cupped hand. The recent gunplay wasn't going to deter them but they rode with guns in hand.

Wade looked around warily, the taut unsmiling expression settling back on his face. The younger man led the way through a yellow gully which eventually led to another stretch of flatland. Across this area of heat-hazed ground was the rocky wall of a high mesa. They rode across at speed and then, close to the cliff stopped to blow the horses.

"This is the City of Ghosts," explained Tommy. "See the cave-mouths and carvings above that ledge? Hundreds of years old! Those ancient Indians had a civilisation of sorts, by all the tales I've heard. If you care to look at the caves you'll see more carved images and pillars and arches. That cliff face is really the remains of an old city. Most of the steps that were cut into the cliff to give access to the caves have crumbled with time, as you can see."

"These carvings link up with the markings in the yellow canyon," muttered Wade. "Queer!"

"You figure we should search those caves?"

"That would take a week, an' what good will it do unless we have something specific to find? I think this old place — almost as old as time and certainly a brooding-place long before the white man came here — connects with the canyon where your pa was killed but I don't understand it at this moment. There's a lack of evidence, Tommy. Just this similarity of old Injun markings. Wal, guess we've seen all we can take in for one ride."

And with a last glance at the silent caves in the old mesa face, they turned the horses for home.

They rode back through the canyon

of death, as it seemed to them now, the place where William Camden and Mac Heggety had died, and then they took to the trail back to Laredo.

It was when they were still two miles out of the town, and on the rutted trail that swept through the Shasta valley, that they saw the sheriff. He was slowly riding a puffing bronc, and he had fixed his gaze on them from a long way off.

"Howdy, Sheriff. Your nag is sure blowing . . ." commented Wade.

Bill Hapner looked critically at the two dusty riders. "Yeah, you don't miss much. Yep, I've been riding fast after a galoot but he tricked me going through the mesquite bush. And you two? You've been pokin' around, huh?"

"We've been shot at by Rip Heggety," Tommy blurted out.

"Now ain't that fun!"

"I showed Wade the canyon where my father was killed and then guns started popping."

"Wal, what do you want me to

do?" barked the sheriff. "Can't you see I've got my hands full with every lawless gent in town! I can't go around warning every doggone gunslinger to quit." Bill Hapner shot a disgruntled look along the trail. "I'm riding back to town. Are you two riding with me?"

The ride back was slow because the sheriff's mount was tired and Bill Hapner was not disposed to hurry. He spent a lot of time, in fact, grousing about his job and the folks of Laredo. Wade grinned and suffered the tirade, glancing now and then at Tommy.

Once into town, they halted outside the sheriff's office as Bill Hapner hitched his animal to the tie-rail. As Wade and Tommy sat their saddles another man cantered a horse up. He was Dave Latimer and his honest face lit up with a smile. He rode his bay close to Wade Tulane and the young fellow — and then hailed the sheriff.

"Howdy, folks! This is sure a grand morning for me. Just made a deal with the railroad company about shipping my beef. Say, railroading is better than a slow trail-herd job. It don't run all the flesh off the critturs!"

Dave Latimer dismounted, stepping to the boardwalk. He turned to Wade and Tommy. "Say, come on inside Bill's office and have a parley. Bill won't mind — that right, you old badge-toter?"

"Sure. Use my office as a goldarned saloon."

Dave Latimer laughed loudly. "Never mind him. I'd like to hear the news . . ."

"I'd sure like to eat," commented Wade.

"Aw, that can wait. There's a lot I'd like to hear."

Tommy Camden got down from the saddle. "All right. Guess I've got ten minutes more to waste. I can tell you, Mr Latimer, how Wade has helped me . . ."

"Just moseying around," began Wade. "We're trying to find out why the Heggety brothers wanted to buy our store," interposed Tommy.

Dave Latimer nodded. "Sure. Come inside this old John Law's office and sit down an' chat."

They all went inside the sheriff's office in a good humour and managed to find seats. Wade found himself beside Bill Hapner's battered old desk. The sheriff brought out his carefully-hoarded bottle of whisky and poured three glasses.

"Reckon you ain't qualified to drink whisky, young feller," he barked at Tommy. "And I ain't the one to start you off!"

The young man blinked and seemed a bit peeved. For the hundredth time recently he wished he had another couple of years on his tally. He was at a bad age, he figured. Men like Bill Hapner reckoned he was still a kid!

There was five minutes of general discussion, which enlightened Dave Latimer considerably with regard to Rip Heggety and his lawless activites.

Bill Hapner was the hardy, restless

type who could not sit at a desk for very long, so he got up and stared through a window at the street-scene. A stage was waiting outside an hotel. At a word from Bill Hapner, Dave Latimer joined him and together they watched some passengers collect around the stage preparatory to boarding for the journey. It seemed that the two men knew some of the passengers and were interested in their activities.

"See that cuss?"

"Yep. You'll be glad to see him out of town, Bill . . . "

Wade Tulane was not very much concerned with the personalities of Laredo, except those who were affecting him at the moment, and he stayed in his seat beside the desk and smoked a cigarette he had rolled from gear the sheriff had offered him.

Tommy Camden got up and crossed to the window and he, too, was seemingly interested in the folks departing by stage that morning.

At that moment Bill Hapner's deputy

entered the office and slapped a large envelope down on the desk. Then, on second thoughts, he picked it up again and slit it open.

"Been to the post-office," he said cordially to Wade. "Ain't nothin' much except these wanted notices. Plenty of them these days."

The deputy did not see the tension in Wade's face. The man was too busy leafing through a number of sheets which were pinned together. As the man flipped casually through them, Wade let his cigarette smoulder between his fingers.

The deputy barely glanced at the sheets. He was about to slip them back into the envelope when a hail came from Bill Hapner.

"Hey, Chad — come over here an' see who's leaving on the stage with the Fenton widow!"

The deputy could not resist this titbit of information and he joined the others at the window. Wade stared at the wanted notices, then reached out a hand while he kept a wary eye on the others at the window.

"You know the stage will have to fold up afore long," said Dave Latimer. "The railroad will get all the trade . . . "

"That ain't so," drawled Bill Hapner. "Some folks don't like railroads. What if them cars come off the rails at that terrible speed — nigh on twenty-five miles an hour? Huh! Ain't no stage do that speed!"

"The railroad for me," remarked Tommy.

"Wal, I do my travellin' on a hoss," said the deputy.

Wade leafed quietly through the wanted notices, no one watching him. He scanned them grimly, intently, one by one, but swiftly. He flicked a glance at the men at the window. They were deriving amusement in watching the stage, something that was always interesting in a town like Laredo.

Wade paused at one sheet. His lips thinned to a tight line. His name stared up at him — but without a picture!

He worked swiftly and silently after that, wasting not another second, slipping the pin out. He detached the wanted sheet and then pinned the others together again. Silently folding the sheet that bore his name, he did not take his eyes off the others at the window, noticing they were laughing at the activities outside. He slipped the sheet into his shirt pocket, in a grim mood, then he glanced again, very casually, at the wanted sheets, and was doing that when Bill Hapner turned, an amused grin on his lips.

It did not alter as he approached Wade, not even when he realised Wade had seen the wanted posters. "Heck, are you interested in them outlaws?"

"Sometimes a man can pick up bounty money," muttered Wade.

"Yeah — an' sometimes get a slug in his gut for his trouble."

The deputy turned. "Those notices just come in, Bill."

"Yeah. I guessed that. Knew you'd

been out for the mail . . . "

The sheriff barely glanced through the sheets and, shaking his head in disgust at this prospect of further trouble, he opened a drawer and pushed the annoying notices out of sight.

Wade shuffled restlessly. "Maybe we ought to be moving, Tommy. I got a feeling we ought to look over your store and try and figure out why the Heggety men were so mighty keen to buy you out. Unless you don't want me nosing around?"

"Why, sure, Wade. You can poke around as much as you want if we can discover why those two ruffians ransacked the house and store."

"Maybe I can help?" offered Dave Latimer.

"Yeah. Stella will be pleased to see you, Mr Latimer."

On this note they left the sheriff and his deputy to their routine business, Wade riding along in silence with the other two. They came slowly down the dusty, busy main stem until the drapery store was reached and there they hitched the animals to a convenient rail.

Stella Camden was busy serving two old ladies when they walked through the store to the living-quarters at the back. She could not leave the ladies at that moment because they seemed bent upon combining gossip with their shopping. Tommy showed Wade and Dave Latimer into the room and indicated chairs.

"Don't know that we should be just sitting around," muttered Wade. He looked appreciatively at the comfortable room, for a fleeting second understanding that Stella liked nice homely things like a real woman should. Wade's eyes lighted on a bureau and he asked: "Have you been through all your pa's effects, Tommy?"

The young fellow nodded. "Sure. We had to check through everything when Stella decided to keep on running the business."

"You didn't find anything that might

interest two toughs like the Heggety brothers?"

"Nothing here. Pa never had any truck with those two jaspers to the best of my knowledge. Nope — just wasn't anything to connect us with those two men."

"And I guess you didn't find anything of unusual interest — I mean something you couldn't explain — something your pa wouldn't usually be mixed in?"

Tommy shook his head, eyes fixed thoughtfully on the Indian rug. "Just wasn't anything unusual, Wade. Oh, I've thought about all those things since the place was ransacked."

"I guess you would . . . just going over the facts, that's all. Was the bureau ransacked?"

"Yeah — how did you suspect?"

Wade smiled. "I've a hunch it belonged to your pa — that right?"

"Yep. Sure, it was open and the papers mussed around — but nothing was missing. In fact, as I've said, nothing was missing from the house or the store."

"They didn't rob you of anything?"

"No. There was some money in the store till. Could have taken that — but they didn't."

Wade felt puzzled. "I'm sure they were looking for something that was hidden by your father. That something is still probably hidden somewhere here. Figures, don't it? Mac and Rip Heggety started out by trying to buy the premises — evidently reckoning that was the easiest way to find this somethin'. When you wouldn't sell, they did what was typical of them — they ransacked the place. And still didn't find what they sought."

"Those two gents were not exactly gentle with the premises," commented Dave Latimer. "They roughed things up. No — they did not find what they wanted — particularly as Stella and Tommy caught them at it. Can't get a notion of what it was they searched for!"

Wade glanced around restlessly. “There’s somethin’ hidden in this house or store. I’ve got a hunch your pa hid this something and the Heggety boyos got to know about it — or just had a suspicion, same as me.”

“But that hellion Rip doesn’t exactly know where to look,” murmured Tommy.

Wade walked around the living-room. He looked intently at the clapboard walls and at the massive stone fireplace. He saw the high mantelpiece on which stood many little ornaments of Indian origin. Two old shotguns were fastened to a wall in a crosswise fashion.

“Any hiding-places in this building? You know — forgotten holes or corners?”

“Well, no. Pa wasn’t the kind of man to hide things, anyway. He was a tidy man — you know, a place for everything and everything in its place! But if you want to start a search, Wade, by all means let us look.”

"That's what I was getting at. We'll start with that chimney. Never can tell . . . "

The three men were ready to start on anything that might solve the mystery and they began by inspecting the inside of the wide chimney. At that time of the year they weren't running a fire. Although Wade dislodged some loose cement, there was nothing strange to see. He knew, of course, that the Heggety brothers must have taken a good look at the chimney during their unlawful search, so that was a futile operation in a sense. Wade turned and tested the floorboards of the living-room, tapping with his boot at various parts, although Indian rugs covered a great deal of the floor.

Tommy and Dave Latimer were examining some of the roof beams. While they were at this work, Stella entered the room, having got rid of her customers.

"Well, what goes on?"

"A search, Sis. We're trying to find

what it was the Heggetys were after."

"It's an idea. How about the bedrooms and the kitchen?"

After some minutes the search became a matter for silent determined work. Wade took up the rugs — with Stella's permission! Tommy went to his bedroom and began examining nooks and corners where he had never thought of looking. Dave Latimer actually went outside the premises, to the stable, and made a search there. Stella looked with unusual intentness at her bedroom. If there was a mystery object to be located in this house they were determined to discover it.

Even as they worked, Wade realised that the Heggety men could have ransacked the house on false assumptions. On the other hand there might be something to be discovered.

While he was testing a part of the flooring he thought most of it seemed to be very solid but there was one part which moved under pressure from his boots. A loose board, no less.

He used a poker for the task of prising up the floorboard. He was well aware that many old-timers favoured the space under floors as a secure hiding-place so it was a good bet to take a look. Anyway, if they searched the house this way and still discovered nothing of value it would eliminate that element from the mystery.

The board was not difficult to ease up. Wade wondered why it was slack when all the other planks were more than secure. This length of board was very short, about a foot in length, which was an unusual feature of a floor in any case.

The mystery was resolved when he discovered a lined space below. He thrust a hand cautiously down into the space, about eighteen inches to be exact. Then bare earth. He sank his arm into the hole and felt around. Nothing!

It seemed these efforts were to no avail. Damn! What was this hole for, anyway, if not a hiding-place?

He drew his hand up again and only as a last measure felt along the underside of the flooring. The pine boards were very rough, scratching his hand. Still nothing!

He was about to give up when his fingers lightly touched something that swung — seemed to move — under the impact of his searching hand.

He soon realised it was a small leather bag tied to a nail. He pulled the thing away, stared at it — and knew this must surely be what they were seeking!

The soft little leather bag was light, a pouch. Maybe it was empty. He didn't believe that for more than a second. This bag had been hidden purposely.

Then he gave a shout to the others. He stood up, holding the bag. "Look at this. A little pouch of leather, tied to a nail. You didn't know it was there, did you — Tommy — Stella?"

"Gawd, no. Do you think this is . . . "

"The thing the Heggetys wanted? We'll find out . . . " Wade handed it to Tommy. "Heck, it's yours — belonged to your pa, I guess."

The young fellow accepted the bag wonderingly. "I don't get it. Why should Pa hide this? What's it all about?"

"Open it," directed Wade.

The lad slackened the cord and opened the bag and then slowly took out the contents. There was a sheet of paper, nothing else. Which had been carefully folded. Tommy smoothed it out and then stared at it. "A map!"

"Does it mean anything?" asked Wade.

"No. I don't understand . . . "

"Open it — smooth it further — take a looksee."

The young fellow slowly attended to the map while Wade stamped the board back into place in the floor.

Tommy called the others together. "Look at this. What do you make of it, Wade? It's done in ink — and it's my pa's work, I'm sure. Look at that writing, Stella."

They crowded round, Dave Latimer joining them staring at the map, intrigued, as well they might be.

"Looks mighty like a map of a canyon," Wade said. "Carefully done, too. See those instructions! It would show anyone how to locate the place, I guess . . . "

Dave Latimer was the first to understand fully. "Good heavens, it's a map of the canyon where William Camden was found dead!"

"Now that beats all," exclaimed Wade. "But it don't surprise."

On the bottom of the sheet was some wording which ran as follows: "Siomi Indian caves. Main entrance located as per map. Note Indian markings on canyon wall. Rock-falls have completely closed the caves. The gold has been buried for centuries. It can stay there until I decide what to do."

In utter silence the party of four scanned the message and stared in astonishment at the fatal map. Slowly, the whole concept sank into their minds.

"Gold!"

"Men will kill for gold," muttered Dave Latimer.

Wade tightened his lips, knowing the absolute truth of those grim words. He remembered his so-called partner — and the wanted notice now in his pocket!

So it was gold that the Heggety men had been after — gold, the metal that led to evil actions by evil men! Those two had killed William Camden for the gold — although the details that had led to the killing were not quite clear.

"I don't understand how — how — Pa made this map — how he knew about this secret gold," said Stella, catching her breath. "Pa wasn't a gold-hunter — or a treasure-hunter . . . "

"You can say he was against the gold-fever, Sis," added the lad. "He didn't like the lawless mob that gold was bringing to Laredo."

"Then how did he learn about these caves?"

"That's a little mystery which I reckon will come out into the light of day sooner or later," said Wade, and he moved away from the table. Just to look at the sheet of paper reminded him of the damned wanted poster in his shirt pocket. He would have to burn it at the earliest opportunity — and hope that another copy did not arrive at the sheriff's office.

"Now we know why those Heggetys wanted to buy you up lock, stock and barrel," he said. "They knew about this gold. Just their meat! They knew William had this map. But how? Aw, it will all become clear."

"If we could prove they shot your pa, we might swing that remaining hellion, Rip Heggety — legally," continued Wade.

"We'll get around to that," Dave Latimer nodded.

Tommy, like a young man, grabbed at the map and swung impulsively to

Wade, eyes bright. "Let's ride out to that canyon and see if we can locate these caves!"

"Heck — hold it," smiled Wade.

Tommy was full of excitement. "Why, this map of Pa's shows the same spot in the canyon we were looking at just this morn! It all adds up. There must be an old hidden cave in that canyon! Looks like it's a relic of the old lost tribe. Can't say I've ever heard of any living Siomi Indians."

"Nor me," added Dave Latimer.

Wade swung round. "Just take it easy, young feller. You want us to go tearing out there with pick an' shovel?"

"Wal, if there's gold . . . "

Wade felt the gun at his side; knew that gold and gunplay went side by side. "There's also Rip Heggety. Somewhere around — maybe watching us right now. He rides a hard trail. He wants this gold, and he also hankers to kill me — and I figure he'll kill you as soon as he grabs that map; if he ever does

. . . Although you salivated his brother, I figure he's laid off you because he thought you'd give him a clue to this map and gold as long as you were alive and breathing."

"I'm not scared of him . . . "

"No. But take things easy. Your pa wasn't in any hurry to go digging for that cave."

"You mean we shouldn't do anything about it?"

Wade grinned at his indignation. "I didn't say that. Matter of fact, the decision is yours because your pa has left you that map . . . It's legally yours, I reckon."

"This discovery is pretty much powerful stuff," commented Dave Latimer.

"I tell you what," interposed the girl. "Let's have something to eat and we can discuss what to do over a meal. Thanks to you, Wade, we've at least achieved something."

"Aw, you'd have gotten round to searching the place yourself."

But the girl was determined, like a good housewife, that the men should have a full meal, and she set to work in the kitchen. Tommy went out to attend a customer in the store. Later, over the meal, the girl learned about the shooting at the canyon and how they had looked at the City of Ghosts.

Then they made plans to ride out and inspect the canyon again, mostly to please the impetuous young lad, with a view to finding the entrance to the old Siomi Indian caves. Dave Latimer offered to help Wade and Tommy, taking guns as well as picks and shovels.

They were busy at the stable behind the store for some time and then they rode out.

Stella Camden thought it wiser to stay behind. It was a bad decision but she was not to know that at the time.

9

Dirty Moves

LEO SANDS watched the three riders leave town. He stood on a boardwalk, smoking a cigarette, almost eating the weed in a sullen mood. From behind a convenient corner he stared savagely at Wade Tulane as he rode away. The man's pale face, hardly affected by summer sun and winds, twisted in a sneer.

His brain juggled with many thoughts, wondering where the three were heading. He noticed the picks and shovels tied alongside the saddles and another sneer crossed his face. Were these lot adding to the mugs working the claims on the river?

If that was true, Rip Heggety might like to know about it! He turned away, throwing his cigarette to the dusty roadway. He thought he would get his horse and take a looksee around.

Maybe this was a chance for Rip Heggety to even up with this Tulane swine and Tommy Camden. Rip sure hated Tulane, and Tommy Camden had killed Mac Heggety. If Rip could get around to throwing lead he might eliminate those two. If fact, if he salivated Dave Latimer in the process all the better. The rancher was too blamed bossy where Stella Camden was concerned, and with him out of the way the set-up would be even more improved.

Leo Sands went to his livery, motivated by his in-bitten thoughts. He got his horse and trotted out of town. He naturally took the trail that led to the mining activities, and he almost caught up with Wade Tulane, Dave Latimer and Tommy but he took care to hang back and he saw them fork off the trail where one tract led to the river and the other out over the desert. Leo Sands stared after the disappearing riders. So they were not bound for the mining camps? Why then were they carrying picks and shovels?

He didn't quite understand but he knew they were taking the desert trail. Maybe Rip Heggety would like to hear about this?

If Rip wanted it that way, he could hit the saddle pretty fast and take his hoglegs along to a shooting-match when he caught up. And Heggety had pals of a similar nature, so he shouldn't be lost for guns if they were needed. And the man could use a Winchester to advantage, he had heard.

Leo Sands rowelled his horse again. Good thing the other three riders had not seen him.

And there was another point of intense interest — at least to his mind. Stella Camden must have been left behind in Laredo! Now that was cute! And without the three guys who apparently would protect her!

He'd ride to the mining-camp, see what was feasible, and he'd ride fast back to town, wasting little time, and pay the girl a visit. He licked his lips. Yeah, that's what he'd do!

In the meantime the three men jogged along at a moderate lope, the sort of pace good horses could maintain all day if needed. The ten miles to the canyon did not constitute an arduous ride.

Eventually, they cantered into the yellow canyon where the silence held, the animals avoiding the clumps of cactus and the weirdly-shaped Joshua trees, prickly pear and boulders. They went right up to the canyon wall where the strange old Indian markings were visible. The three men stared at the hieroglyphics, not that they could make any sense out of these mysterious signs and symbols. Winds and rains of centuries had scoured them and only a scholar could decipher them.

Wade said: "This is where you use that map, Tommy. Seems like there ought to be an entrance to a cave around here . . . "

Tommy got his map out, flattened it against his saddle. "Gosh, I'd like to find the gold!"

"Reckon it brings nothing but grief," said Dave Latimer. "Your pa knew that truth judging by the way he hid the map."

Wade nodded. "That's something else we got to figure out. How's your father get that map? I mean, of course, the information to draw it out? Wal, we'll find that out some day. And another thing — how come he was sure there'd be gold in these lost Indian caves?"

"A mystery," said Dave Latimer. "He did not confide in me — and I was an old friend. But we won't worry about that . . . the main job is to locate these durned Indian caves."

Wade stared along the canyon wall and at the Indian markings. "Accordin' to the map we've got to note the markings. Wal, we sure have noted them but I reckon they take some studying. Do you see any sign, young feller? Of a cave, I mean . . . "

"Not here. There are some in the City of Ghosts, but that's way off from here. The map points to this canyon wall and going by the drawing Pa made, the mouth should be about there." And the young man pointed to a spot just left of the scoured Indian hieroglyphics. The three men stared, each with his own thoughts: Wade with a bitter smile, remembering the gold he'd panned for in Colorado and lost; Dave Latimer wisely keeping his own judgement, and Tommy full of eagerness.

The canyon wall to which the lad had pointed seemed solid, although it was very jagged in parts and there was an accessible slope on which fallen rock had heaped.

"We've got a helluva job on hand, amigos," snapped Wade. "Looks like we ought to get down from the saddle an' start digging an' poking around."

"We might be lucky," jerked Tommy. "We'll start on the exact spot that the map pin-points."

The eagerness of the young reporter was refreshing. They took the gear from the saddles and began climbing the rough face. The lad might be right at that. If the map was accurate, there was a cave behind that apparently solid heap of jagged rock, an age-old cave used by the Siomi Indians.

They ground-hitched the horses before they started and they took water-canteens. The afternoon sun was fierce, the yellow sand throwing back the heat, and they would need water if they were going to work hard.

The three men started on the approximate spot indicated on the map as the position of a cave-mouth. The first major chore was to prise away a big boulder, which involved a lot of work. This took their combined efforts and, sweating profusely, they only stopped when the boulder rolled clear and they needed some refreshing water.

"Kinda hot work with this blamed

sun." Wade straightened his back. "Might be better to work at night — or at least after sundown."

"But we'd waste time . . . "

"Time is a mighty strange factor," commented Wade, "Seeing as how we're talking about a possible cave that's centuries old."

"But Heggety will learn about this place. He could come spying around at any time . . . "

"Well, let him."

"Just that he has some hardy cusses palling up with him right now."

"We're tough hombres, too," grinned Wade.

"I'd like a chance to swap lead with that man," snapped Tommy.

Wade ruffled the young lad's hair. "Goddam it, you sound like a gunslinger — and you are not. Let's get on with the digging."

"Yeah — we should forget Rip Heggety. After all, we're three guns to his one — even if Tommy is not yet a gunny!" And Dave laughed at his joke.

While they were talking they little realised that Leo Sands had met up with the man they were discussing at the placer camp and got Heggety really interested. So much so that the snarling man had called Dutch from his work and told him to get the horses.

"You say those men had picks and shovels, Mister Sands?"

"Yep. Went out by the desert trails . . . "

"They did, huh? That's to the yellow canyon . . . " Rip Heggety fingered his unshaven face and scowled thoughtfully. "Wal, thanks for the news, amigo. Me an' Dutch will hit leather."

"Kill them," muttered Leo Sands. "Remember Tommy Camden shot your brother."

"I don't need reminding." He sneered. "You are still hankerin' for that gal, huh! Hell, if I wanted a bitch that bad I'd just carry her off. But you can find women in the saloons . . . "

"Every man to his own way," said

Leo Sands smoothly. "Maybe you've got ideas why those three are riding out with mining tools? The desert ain't gold country. The gold is in the river."

"Not always," sneered Rip Heggety. "Now outa my way, feller. Hey, Dutch, are you going to be all day with them hosses!"

"Jus' about ready," mumbled the big man, and he yanked on the cinch of his own big mare.

Leo Sands rode out of the mining-camp well satisfied with the trend of events. He had little doubt that Heggety and his pard would overtake Tulane and his friends. Maybe colt lead would fly. Maybe rifle fire would settle Wade's past for good, with a stealthy bullet fired at distance, if Heggety had any sense.

He hoped the three men who stood between him and the girl would hit the dust and stay there!

He rode at a fast lick back to town, watered the animal when it was evident that was needed, and then took himself into a saloon to down a few shots of whisky as a preliminary to his main course of action.

He came out, wasting no more time, and walked his horse slowly along to the drapery emporium and hitched the creature to the tie-rail. He crossed the boardwalk and boldly entered the store.

Stella came to the counter, the place being empty, and she halted on seeing Leo Sands. "You!"

"Me!" grinned the gambling man. "Just figured to pay a visit, Stella."

"Please, I don't want to talk — or see you."

"That ain't no way to speak to me."

"Please don't make this unpleasant. You know I don't want your attentions. Now please go."

"Not so damned quick," snapped Leo Sands, losing his temper. "I know your brother and that damned Tulane guy are not around. They rode out of town with Latimer."

"Oh, you saw them. That's why you're here." Stella instinctively backed away.

"I want to talk to you alone," said the gambler. He made an effort to be civilised. "You know I want to marry you, Stella. That's something, isn't it? I aim to be an important man in this town and you could come along with me — give me background — the other women in town accept you."

"You — a gambler! I wouldn't marry you. Can't you accept that?"

"Some men look up to me." His voice thickened with anger.

"Well, I don't. Now go."

"You've got eyes for that blamed stranger, Tulane."

"That's not for you to say," flared the girl, a blush on her cheeks.

"I know it. I can read you. Wal, he'll get his," said Leo Sands evilly. "The whole blamed lot of 'em will get a bellyful of lead — pretty soon — ah — "

He realised he had said too much in

his rush of anger as he saw the girl's eyes widen in fright. "You saw them ride out — and you know something!"

"Forget it."

"They're riding into a trap," breathed the girl. "Isn't that it?" Instincts had supplied the answer if not the details.

"You are giving me crazy talk, girl. I didn't say that . . . "

"But it's true. I can guess — by your manner." And Stella, hardly knowing more than this hunch, turned and ran into the living-room at the rear of the store.

She had a swift notion to saddle a horse and ride out after the others, to warn them.

Goaded into actions that even he knew were a blunder, Leo Sands followed the girl. He grabbed her and held her, his strength superior to hers. It was the first time he had touched the girl, held her in his grasp, and the sensations aroused everything savage in him. She struggled and gave a sharp scream.

"Cut it out! That won't do any good. And don't fight me — just say you'll be mine." He struggled with her, aware of her soft roundness. "Just promise that."

"You are mad."

"You'll be mighty glad to turn to me when you're all alone. Guess you'll need a man then, my girl!"

"You are awful. Let me go!"

"Nope! I love you!"

"That's madness!" she breathed. "You don't know the meaning of the words!"

"I'll show you . . . " And his mouth sought her lips, savagely, without kindness, just a bad urge to subdue her.

She fought him and her strength was about equal to his because he was a young man who had never worked any harder than to shuffle a deck of cards.

She jerked out words while she fought. "You expect Wade and Tommy to be killed! That's the truth! Oh,

God — I must warn them! Let me go!"

The struggle began in real earnest because, aware that he had made admissions that might be troublesome, he hardly knew what he was doing; but on second thoughts he was sure a few fool words couldn't be used against him. When the three who had ridden into the desert were dead, words wouldn't be of much account!

However, he didn't intend to allow the girl to go running out of the store and into the busy street. He wanted to impress her, bend her to his will, in fact. He'd show her he'd be her master.

His actions were running out of control. The things got out of hand as the girl, possessed with righteous anger, struck out at him. She struck his face, drawing blood, something that made him hiss in anger. It was more by accident that Leo Sands stumbled. She ran quickly from the room in the few seconds available to her, freeing herself from his attack in a fast movement.

She rushed out into the rear yard and then into the street. Blindly, she just knew she had to escape this man.

10

Man Down

SHE ran and ran, instinctively towards the sheriff's office along the busy main drag, with no one giving her more than a curious glance although ladies usually did not run. With every yard she covered she blessed her luck in escaping from the man. He was stupidly impossible! What right had he to believe she liked him, let alone anything else!

She'd complain to the sheriff. Bill Hapner would know how to deal with the fool of a man!

It was pretty easy for Leo Sands to guess the girl was heading for the sheriff's office and he cursed his luck. He halted on the boardwalk. Then he swung around and grabbed at his horse. He realised he had made a fool-play in approaching the girl the way he had. Things had got out of control; better to take a breather.

He did not wish to explain himself to the sheriff although it wasn't a crime to approach a pretty girl and make a pass! That was all he had done — so far. But he knew he wanted to take her, to have the lovely creature in any way, violently if need be! In fact, it might be fun to conquer her that way!

It was better to light out now and hope that events in the desert would go the way he wanted. Then he'd see finally about this girl. He'd get her, by thunder he would!

By the time Stella found Bill Hapner and poured out her story to him, Leo Sands had ridden out of town. He had little intention of riding to the desert, where there might be gunplay, because that was not his line. He did not want to act until he heard from Rip Heggety and Dutch. He would lie low and hope his enemies might die of lead poisoning.

Stella had grabbed Bill Hapner's arm when she found him. "Leo Sands has been pestering me! But worse than that — I can put up with that, though he was really terrible — he gave me a hint that Tommy and Wade and Dave Latimer are riding into a trap."

"Huh? Where've they gone?"

"They are riding out to the canyon where Pa was found dead. Probably they are there now. Leo Sands has stirred up something for them, I'm sure."

"Why in heck are they out there?"

"We made a discovery in our house, Sheriff. There's hidden gold in that canyon . . . "

"Shucks, gal — no gold in the desert around here — just the river — they ought to know that."

"We found a map made by Pa." And she outlined the situation. The sheriff whistled. "Gold! Indian gold, huh! There's always grief where there's gold. But where's this pesky Leo Sands? I'll go kick his hide."

And Bill Hapner stamped out into the main drag of Laredo with the girl in tow, his anger impressive, but the young gambling-man had vanished. The sheriff returned to the drapery store with the girl. She began locking up for the day while the sheriff stared grimly up and down the street in case he could sight Leo Sands. Then Stella went to the stables at the back of the premises and led out her horse.

"I'm riding out after my brother and Wade and Mr Latimer. I reckon to warn them — if I'm not too late."

"Just a moment, gal. I can't just allow you to ride alone if there's danger — but dammit I'm busy with other things. Still, I'll mosey along with you. Just give me chance to get my nag — and I guess you can explain more as we take that trail. One thing is for sure, there's plenty of time . . . "

Stella smiled. "Thanks, Sheriff . . . I know you have plenty of troubles on hand but we must hurry. We could be too late. I'm scared."

"Those three can tackle danger as it come along. Wal, I'll ride out with you because I'd like to know more about all this."

He did not waste much time in joining the girl in the main stem because his nag was saddled and fresh, with a rifle in the scabbard. With a final glance around at the activity in Laredo's main drag, he rode out swiftly with the girl.

On the ride she told the lawman about the finding of the map which showed the whereabouts of the long-lost cave in the yellow canyon. Stella thought it best to tell the man everything because he was a friend and, as the law, could be trusted. Then they urged the animals into a fast lope. Soon they were heading into arid terrain where few other riders were encountered.

In the meantime, Wade Tulane and the others were making good progress towards uncovering the position of the cave-mouth. They rolled huge stones to one side, pausing to drink as the heat got to them.

And then it happened, the silence of the land violated. A shot cracked through the yellowstone canyon and sent a burst of dust up near Wade's feet. He didn't need to be told the shell came from a rifle. And when another three shots bit into dirt all around them they had a pretty good hunch who was firing. All three men darted to cover behind large boulders. And they blessed the fact that the attackers were in a heck of a hurry to shoot and thereby spoiling their aim!

"Rip Heggety!" snapped Wade. "Who else?"

"And a pal or two," supplied Dave Latimer. "More than one rifle here . . . he's durned fast in locating us . . . that man seems to spend most of his time getting at you, Wade."

The three men stared grimly across the silent floor of the yellow sands of the canyon. The first shots had been intended as a drygulch shot or two, with the intent to kill, but the attackers were in too great a hurry and had botched the job. Now there was no chance of surprise and the gunnies had fallen silent. Maybe they were working their way to a better vantage point.

Wade stared at the canyon wall and the jumble of broken rock at the base. Men could easily hide among that pile-up of boulders and rock chunks, and with a rifle they could reach across to a target.

The next moment, as if in answer to his thoughts, two rifles spoke from the other side and dust spat as the bullets bit into rock inches from Wade and Tommy. As the echoes died away, Wade shouted: "Two of 'em!"

"Kinda long range for our Colts." Dave Latimer crouched down. "No use wasting slugs over that distance . . . "

"They've got our range but they're not very accurate." Wade stared for a sight of movement.

"Well, we just can't sit here," yelled Tommy.

"Don't you move, young feller."

"But — but — we should be getting at 'em!"

"Take it easy. *I'm* going out to hunt those galoots — not you."

"I could help."

"You and Dave can cover me with a fusillade of shots," retorted Wade. "I figure that will keep those damned nuisances ducking down although you won't hit them at this long range. And we're a long way off our nags so — "

"We'll cover you," promised Dave Latimer.

"I want to get up this canyon wall further, right to the top, and make a way and get around the dead end. Maybe I can get near to those gun-happy galoots and drop them."

"But you're taking all the chances," objected the young lad.

"I've been doing that for a long time," Wade grinned back. "And I might get away with it once more. Those two galoots ain't so good, anyway. They don't know how to use a smokepole, I reckon. Now give those galoots a hail of lead — Tommy — Dave — ”

As the shooting started, he dashed for the jagged cover of the rocks, flinging a couple of shots across the canyon floor in the hope that they would add to the deterrent. However he had to holster his Colt so that he could use both hands as well as his feet in the climb up the wall. He darted through small crevices and hauled himself up rough ledges without a pause. The guns now below him cracked the air. A couple of shots whistled past his head and dug into rock, sending chips and dust flying into his face. Then he reached the top and darted into a long but shallow crevice which extended for some distance. A few minutes later he considered he was reasonably clear of danger. He was intent upon getting around to the dead end of the canyon so that he'd be on the other side of the attackers. He figured to creep up on them and see how they liked Colt fire in return.

He scrambled further along the top of the canyon wall, almost on the ridge, with plenty of cover, a crouched figure most of the time. He jumped from rock to rock, dodging the prickly pear and hoping he would not disturb a rattler. He rounded the dead end and began to work his way down the rocky wall in which Rip Heggety and his pal were hidden. That the would-be killer was the Heggety slob he had no doubt!

Wade went through a slit almost filled with cholla cactus, the spikes tearing at his clothes, but that was the least of his troubles. He stepped up on to bare rock at the end of the slit and then dropped down again into a sort of gully, continuing along like that for about twenty yards.

He heard the exchange of shots below him, the echoes whipping across the golden sands of the canyon floor. He grinned. Dave Latimer and Tommy were successfully keeping the other men busy.

Then, grimly, he judged he was close to the position from where Rip Heggety and his side-kick were shooting. He would have to slow down, exercise more care.

He inched along and suddenly sank close to the rock, Colt now in his hand. He saw a head move from behind a boulder — and then dart back again.

"Got you located!" Wade muttered.

There had not been time for a shot. But he had located the men. Grimly he hoped he had the guts to shoot a man in the back, for that was the momentary view he'd got of one of the men. If the chance came again he would have to trigger for the sake of Tommy and Dave Latimer who were not experienced gunmen.

Wade slid forward over the bare slab of rock in order to get the last few inches of advantage. He wondered where the men had hidden their horses. Probably some way back among the natural corrals made by the rocks.

He lay grim and ruthless. He would

kill if faced with the decision. He was sure the chief hellion was Rip Heggety, a man who wanted vengeance. It might be the guy would end his days without that satisfaction!

Wade could hear the sound of his own breathing as he lay close to the hot rock, and as he slid forward yet another inch his belt buckle scraped the rock giving him the feeling that two men down below, among the huddle of boulders, must surely hear his movement.

But they did not. Then there was an intervention that surprised even Wade Tulane. He heard a shout and then the quiet hot air of the canyon thudded to the sound of horses' hoofs. The sound increased with every passing second as he hugged the rock. Then there was another shout as two riders came tearing into the yellow canyon.

Wade raised himself at that moment, narrowed his eyes as he noted instantly that the first rider was a girl — Stella Camden. She was followed by another rider, Bill Hapner!

Even as Wade raised himself, he felt movement by the two men just below him. A man jumped to a boulder and pointed his rifle on the two swiftly-moving riders.

Wade just had enough time to note that this man was not Rip Heggety, and then, with deadly precision, he triggered his gun down at the gunman.

One shot and the man plunged forward, his rifle falling from his grasp as he slowly toppled into the rocks. His strangled cry of pain and oncoming death made another horrible sound in the canyon air. The echoes of the Colt died away. As they faded, Wade heard the rasp of boots on loose rock-chippings and he realised that Rip Heggety was making his escape.

The other man was dead, sure thing. Grimly, he felt some miserable satisfaction in eliminating the man from the scene but not because the guy was dead. Then Wade scrambled to his feet and, crouching, went along the rocky debris on the top of the canyon wall.

That he had saved Stella from a death-shot he was certain that much gave him satisfaction. But he wished the man had been Rip Heggety.

"That rannigan is making me mad!" he muttered. "Damn him to hell! If he was bound for Boot Hill, we'd all be happy."

Wade did see the man momentarily and, as he glimpsed the figure, he fired his Colt. The slug missed, which wasn't surprising in a frantic chase. Then the man loosed off a couple of slugs which forced Wade to duck and slow down. A second later, however, he poked out his gun-arm and fired at the hellion.

With the luck of his kind, Rip Heggety was not hurt. He dashed out of cover and flung himself down a gully between the rocks. Wade heard the sound of the man's movements as boots slithered on loose rock-chips, even the man's gasps and curses.

Wade went forward grimly and without wasting any time because the chase was a matter of life and death, his guns snapping off shots. But too much rashness could easily be dangerous he knew. Heggety's guns were equally as menacing as his own.

It was a grim game of chase among the never-ending spread of rocky debris and boulders, with swift slugs spitting every few seconds. Wade stopped to reload, bitter at all this gunplay, this game of death. Then Wade had his stroke of bad luck.

He slipped badly and fell, striking the side of his head against a protruding knob of rock. With his head wound still sore, this added to the pain. He lay dazed for some seconds during which time Heggety made his getaway, not realising that his enemy was, in fact, temporarily helpless. Had the guy known, a bullet might have ended Wade's life.

But Wade rose unsteadily to his feet, stared around him and then holstered his gun. He realised that Heggety had got the all-important head start. He couldn't see the man, nor could he hear any sound from him.

Wade went on, of course, because he was that kind of determined cuss, moving carefully through the rocky debris. Then the sound of a horse's hoofs on rocky chips and shale came to his ears and he knew that Heggety was making his escape, a lucky man! Wade broke into a run, staggering a bit, moving from rock to rock. But the other man's horse evidently found a way out of this wilderness of rock, for the sound of hoofbeats got further and further away.

Heggety was lighting out! But most probably figuring to craftily return another day.

Wade went back grimly to the spot where he had shot down Heggety's side-kick. He examined the man but could not identify him except to figure he was one of the men from the mining-camp to judge from his clothes. Well, the man had paid the price of friendship with Heggety!

Quickly, grimly, he piled small rocks over the body and then picked up the man's rifle, a badly-scratched Winchester. Wade then discovered a rather tricky path down to the canyon floor and started on this route.

A bit later he walked steadily across the yellow sand on a straight line for the others. They waited, a small bunch, still warily holding guns and staring around. Wade came up, his boots crunching against the sun-baked terrain.

"One dead," he said curtly. He nodded to the sheriff. Then he smiled at the girl. "I don't know why you're here — but I am pleased to see you."

"I found out that you were in danger. Leo Sands came into the store to bother me, and I knew by his words that something bad was planned for you."

"Leo Sands, huh? I might teach him not to bother you some day. What did he say?"

Stella lightly touched his arm. "What

does it matter? You're safe." She turned. "All of you, thank goodness!"

Sheriff Hapner surveyed the work the three men had done on the old cave. Evidence of freshly-disturbed soil and rock debris was everywhere. "So this is the reason for all this gunplay! Gold! Sure recipe for grief! So William Camden died because of this!"

"Yep. This is what Rip Heggety and his brother were after," snapped Wade. "With Boot Hill for one! Now only one left. According to a map William Camden made and left hidden under the floorboards of his house, there should be gold in this cave — but not the new stuff the miners pan from the river or dig out. This is old gold hidden by the Siomi Indians."

"Yeah. Miss Stella told me a lot about it on the ride."

"You nearly rode into an ambush."

Bill Hapner grimaced. "I guess I let Miss Stella have too much headway. She made the pace and I had to follow."

"We tried to warn you about those two hell-bents," said Tommy. "But I reckon you and the sheriff didn't understand our shouts, Stella."

"How about getting on with the work now, Wade?" Tommy Camden was still eager.

"Wish I could stop to wash and eat," said Wade wryly. "But we'll have to stick around until we discover something. Rip Heggety won't be far off. He knows the score. He might be back with another gold-hungry hellion."

"You mean we can't leave the site?" exclaimed Dave Latimer.

Wade found time to roll a cigarette. "We'll have to stick around now. Can't leave gold to the vultures!"

Sheriff Hapner scratched his head. "Guess I'll have to ride back to town. I'll have to leave you. I'm the law — but I can't be everywhere." He paused. "But you can rely on me to say nothing about this Injun gold until you got real title to it. I reckon finders is keepers — unless I figure out any other little law."

"We'll get the gold if we can," stated Dave Latimer. "Not that I'm interested because my ranch is more than enough for me. But maybe Stella and Tommy might feel a need to be rich."

"We ain't got it so far," rapped Wade. "Anyway, it don't belong to me . . . "

"Fair enough." The sheriff turned away. "Wal, anybody riding back with me?"

"You ought to go back," said Tommy, looking at his sister.

"And be pestered by Leo Sands?" flashed the girl.

"You could stay with the Grahams — they're good friends of ours. Mick Graham would smash Leo Sands into the ground if you said the word. You'd better get back home, Stella."

"Not me!" flashed the girl and she gripped the headstall of her horse all the firmer. "I'm staying right here until I see that gold."

"If there is any," muttered Wade.

Tommy glanced at the sinking sun. "We might be here all night, Sis."

"I don't care. I've got a saddle-blanket and the sand is warm."

"And what if Heggety returns with gun-happy pals?" asked Wade.

"There'll be four of us — and I notice you've got the dead man's rifle."

"Gosh, you're stubborn," exploded Tommy.

"Just like you, dear," said the girl. "I note you're using that injured arm — so how stubborn can you get?"

And that was the way she influenced the others in allowing her to stay with them in the heat-filled yellow canyon, where anything might happen and gold was present to stir a man's greed.

The sheriff rode away, shaking his head, a man with many problems and a town to run. He could not concern himself entirely with the problems of the two Camdens no matter how friendly he had been in the past.

The girl rounded up the horse that

had strayed during the shooting and they were all tethered near to some satisfying grass, sparse though that growth was in the canyon. Wasting no more of the evening sun, the others set to work, intent on clearing a way into the ancient Siomi cave. After some work it seemed that there was a natural cave behind the rubble. They just had to toil on grimly, hoping that the fall that had blocked and concealed the cave for about two centuries did not extend too far into the actual cave-mouth.

Wade thought: "Damned gold! Why am I doing this? Haven't I had enough trouble with the yellow metal to last me a long time? And what if a duplicate of that wanted poster finds its way to the sheriff's office?"

11

The Bad Deal

WADE TULANE and the other two men worked incessantly, pulling more rock clear of the cave-mouth. This process built up a sort of rampart around the area, something that might be useful if Heggety or indeed any other ruffian decided to get curious about the cave.

But the hard work told on Tommy Camden; he wasn't used to it, and the pain in his shoulder increased. As the sun sank lower, ready to plunge out of sight as it did in these western parts, and the cave-mouth provided nothing of interest in the shape of Indian artefacts or gold, Tommy stopped work on Wade's orders and joined Stella in her position as lookout.

"Better rustle up some grub, Sis. I

reckon everyone is hungry. I'll help you gather some tinder. It won't make any difference about a fire giving our location away because Heggety knows where to find us if he wants to start trouble."

She went to the horses and untied a food-bag. The men had anticipated the need for food and they had coffee and beans, water and two pans and enamel mugs. Stella set up the fire with the aid of some stones to contain it. Then glancing at Wade and Dave Latimer, still toiling in the cave-mouth, and with the light failing, she went beyond the site with Tommy and searched for dry tinder.

This was mostly dead cactus root and greasewood which they found in odd nooks down the slope of the canyon wall.

She went along with her brother but somehow she found herself a fair distance from him. And then Tommy made the mistake of leaving her, returning with his arms full of burning-material and stacking it near the fireplace.

Stella was not actually aware that she was alone and a good distance from where the men were working on the old cave-mouth. She was busy picking up tinder when she sensed movement on her left side. She wheeled around, her mouth opening in shock. But her scream was a tiny thing that was choked off as the man leaped at her and clamped a huge dirty palm over her mouth.

Her struggles availed her little because she was immediately dragged to a rocky hideout, there to be greeted by another sneering devil, Rip Heggety, no less!

"Not another struggle outa you, my beauty!" Heggety's warning was a low hiss. "Come on, Sep, let's move back. I reckon we've got a prize worth holding on to. Right now we're too close to those other rannigans."

The man known as Sep Corry, an unshaven ruffian who admired Heggety, a guy without much mental ability, nodded and gripped the girl cruelly, hauling her back along the rock-lined crevice they had used in order to get close to the cave. Quickly, in spite of the burden of a struggling girl, they went right back along the ragged canyon wall to the cunning hole where they had hidden their horses. It was a recess that could be overlooked a hundred times even by searching men.

"Hold her, Sep! I'll tie her!" Heggety got a length of manila from his saddle and rapidly cut lengths with which he bound the girl. He tore his red bandanna and made a gag. This stopped the girl from screaming the moment Sep Corry withdrew his dirty hand.

"Got her! Now maybe we can use this gal as a trump card!"

"What's the use of a gal?" asked Sep Corry. "Except for one thing . . . " His stupid eyes looked at Heggety.

Heggety laughed. "You'll see, man. An' there's more than one thing, feller!

This girl will be a good swap for a cache of gold! Yeah! Got it, man? That's what those galoots are after, Sep — like I told you. Gold! Old Injun gold. I knew it but I never could figure out where the cave was in this canyon. Now we know . . . "

"I ain't never heard of Injun gold, Heggety."

"You're a dumb bastard," stated Heggety. "But no matter — you're a right useful hombre an' I'll see you all right. This gold is buried in the canyon wall, a cave more'n a hundred years old — maybe older, I dunno. Real gold — better than panning and breaking the back!"

"How'd you know all this, Rip?"

"Old man Camden had the secret, damn him. But he wouldn't talk and got a slug in the back. Maybe that was a bad play because Mac and me could never have found the location of the Indian cave."

Stella's eyes flashed with hatred of this unpleasant man. She was gagged and bound — but she was listening — and hating!

"Mac and me knew Camden got the secret of this Injun gold off an old redman who said he was the last of the old Siomi tribe. This Injun was dying when he told Camden the secret — Gawd knows why. That damned draper-man made a drawing of the location but me and Mac never found it, although he tried to buy the store, thinking that was the easy way. The blamed fools refused to sell so we ransacked the place. Still no dice! Aw, well, we're on to it now, Sep! Ain't no stopping us."

Rip Heggety gave a hearty chuckle.

"Let's git along to them other fellers," slurred Sep Corry. "I reckon we could kill them mighty fast!"

"Yeah? That's your way of thinking. Those cusses ain't so easy, Sep. Wal, I'd sure like to see them dead — particularly that ornery Tulane. He's crossed me too many times."

"Let's git along," snarled the other

man. Stupidly he said: "Hell — there's only one way to get that gold an' that's to shoot for it."

"Right," decided Heggety. "We'll get along to the point in the rocks — near the treasure-cave — but leave things to me, you understand? Maybe we'll shoot to kill — and maybe we'll make a little deal with this gal. She's worth her weight in gold, ain't she?" And Heggety laughed at his joke. "You just take orders, Sep. All right, huh?"

The other man nodded as if he understood, but a defective retentive memory was no asset. Heggety had a partner who could be a liability. Heggety glanced again at the man in the darkening light and sneered inwardly. If Sep was useful for a shooting-match — okay. If he got himself killed — too bad!

Rip Heggety thought that Sep Corry might get killed in any case, sooner or later, because gold was too valuable to split two ways! Leaving the girl gagged and bound in the hidden nook the two hell-bent men set off again along the concealed track to the vantage point near the gold-cave. The sky became dark with the suddenness of this Texas area. This was to the ruffians' good. They reached the last possible stand for them among the rock and boulders and sank into hiding, conferring in whispers.

"Remember, man — you take orders."

"Sure, Rip — I ain't stupid."

"No?" Heggety sniggered.

"I can see a feller. You want I should shoot him now?"

"Hell, no! What's the good of killing one? Just wait, Sep. Maybe we can get a bead on all three of 'em."

"Can't hear any sound of them workin'," grunted Sep Corry.

"It's darkish, that's why . . . "

But there was another reason for the lack of noise. By now Tommy had realised that Stella was missing and he had gasped out the news in dismay to Wade and Dave Latimer.

Wade had spent some minutes

scouring around in the gloom, the rifle held at waist-level, ready to plug the first stranger he encountered. He had gone some way along the canyon, searching the thousands of nooks and hollows but to no effect. He stared around at the eerie shapes of giant rocks that had lain at the base of the canyon wall for centuries. The rocks were round and smooth, the result of winter winds and rain and sandstorms. These grotesque heaps were like sentinels of the night where a man could hide in a hundred places.

With the light faint and gloomy, it seemed a hopeless task just looking for the girl. He felt so strongly about her, he just had to find her. Stella! Her very name now brought an ache to his heart. Where was she? By God, he'd kill any man who got in his way. He knew she had not just got herself lost. Something had happened. Heggety again! He was around, out there in the damned night.

Warily, rifle at the ready, he

backtracked. He went to the camp, where they now had a fire going. Dave and Tommy waited for him, guns in hands, eyes desperately searching the night for shapes.

"No good," Wade muttered. "I just can't sight anyone."

"I shouldn't have allowed her out of my sight!" groaned Tommy.

"She ain't just lost." Dave Latimer felt really angry.

"That means Rip Heggety!" muttered Tommy. "I'll kill him if anything happens to Sis!"

"You might have a chance. There's every possibility of gunplay afore long. Wish I knew where Heggety was hiding . . . "

The three men stood in a gap of the barricade they'd made with rock from the half-explored cave-mouth, and the night air seemed to lighten a bit with the hint of a rising moon. Wade and Dave Latimer walked away from the rampart of rocks and they took slow, wary steps down the jagged canyon wall. They paused every few seconds to stare around. If they saw anything that moved, they were ready to shoot.

It was then that Sep Corry fired, getting a dim idea that Rip Heggety had given the order — which he had not!

The gun lanced flame through the darkness. The slug took away Dave Latimer's hat — an unintentionally good shot from the dim ruffian.

Wade and the rancher dropped flat to the desert and tried to emulate burrowing creatures. Hugging the earth, they watched a cloud sail over the light caused by the moon and the canyon was momentarily darkish again, an eerie silent place now that the echoes from the shot had died away.

Then, running for the comparative shelter of two lone boulders, Wade and the rancher loosed off fast shots at the spot where they had seen the gun-flame. Immediately, more guns flared their flame and smoke, spitting vengeful slugs, but they simply dug holes in the hard sand.

Wade waited for the moonlight to appear again, hugging a small boulder, only his hand poking out holding his six-shooter. The rifle was by his side. He was not discarding it, but the Colt would serve if he could only get a bead on the attacking men.

It was at that moment that Sep Corry made another dim-witted mistake. As the cloud floated away and the sky lightened, the fool of a ruffian rose from behind the rock and aimed his gun at the boulder sheltering Wade Tulane.

Wade snapped off a lightning shot that took the man right between the eyes. The man staggered out of cover, dead on his feet, blood spurting terribly from his face. He fell forward like a log, still and quite dead, blood forming a pool in the yellow sand.

There was an angry shout from Rip Heggety.

"Damn you, Tulane! Keep that gun holstered from now on! You hear me?

I've got the girl! If you want to see her alive again, get back to that cave and start working."

"What's your idea?" Wade snarled.

"I mean I want that gold. Remember I've got the girl. Get back an' work on that cave until you discover all the gold — an' I mean all. You've got enough light from what I can see. Uncover that gold and then clear out — ride away. Then I'll hand over the Camden gal."

"That's some deal," Wade mocked. "You reckon to make us do the work, huh?"

"I know you ain't got that gold uncovered as yet or you'd be loading horses."

"Maybe there ain't any, hombre."

"Quit foolin' me, Tulane. There's all night as yet. Build up that fire an' get to work. I'll be watching . . . "

"Maybe you'd like to come and lend a hand," Wade attempted a trick.

"No sirree! Not unless you galoots figure to throw down your guns — clear of that cave — where I can see. You could do that. I'll settle for either deal." There was a triumphant laugh from Rip Heggety. "Remember, I've got the girl. If you figure to trick me I might just blast her. Maybe I could work that cave myself."

"But you want us to do the chore," mocked Wade.

"Good idea, ain't it?"

"We might blast you."

"That would be too bad, mister clever Tulane. The gal might die of starvation if you couldn't find her after I was dead — and I reckon she's well-hidden. Yeah, she could just lie in that hole and rot if you hombres eliminated me — so don't get too gun-handy!"

Silence fell over the scene for what seemed an eternity to Wade and the others. Then: "All right, Heggety, we'll get to working on the treasure-cave. Maybe we're near to uncovering the hidden gold — I don't know. Maybe there ain't any . . . "

"The hell there ain't."

"We'll make the deal as soon as we break into the cave proper and find that gold. You'll hand over Miss Stella safe and sound. Does that suit you?"

"Yep. Unless you want to throw down your guns. I could join you if you did that — and if I was satisfied you'd done it."

"We don't want your help."

"All right, damn you. Get on working. I'd like you to find that gold. Heh! Heh!" Heggety considered it was time for him to laugh!

"We'll start working if you beat it. We don't want to be shot in the back."

Another laugh rose from the rocks. "All right — I reckon you know what will happen to the gal if you try any tricks. I'm moving back, Tulane — an' if you try to plug me remember the gal might just lie and rot!"

Wade lay flat behind his boulder, grim, his thoughts with Stella, hating the feeling that she might be suffering and fearful. He just wanted to defend her — against anything or anybody. He could not yet analyse his feelings. Why did a man feel like this about a girl — particularly a man like himself?

He heard the sound of boots on loose rubble but saw no sign of the now hateful man. He would have no compunction in this miserable type of man.

The guy was hiding himself well even if he did hold a trump card in the fact that the girl's life could not be risked.

Wade gave Heggety a few minutes, and then he ran across the canyon floor at a crouch, gun at the ready, and he began to climb to the cave site. No shots came his way. Presently Dave Latimer joined him.

"Have we got to work for that swine?" raged the rancher.

"We'll make a play of doing some work because he'll be watching. I figure this is the best move — better than dropping our guns."

"Sure, better than that. But, Wade, how can we best that devil? You've got an idea — I figure you have, amigo."

Tommy Camden joined them. "I heard the shooting. Didn't seem anything I could do . . . "

Wade touched him. "Never rush out where there's shooting. You heard Heggety?"

"Yeah — every word, damn him."

"He's got Stella hidden away someplace. He's right — we might never find her if we kill him." Wade stared grimly at the young fellow. "Set to work, friends. That snake has got to be convinced we're working on the Indian cave and looking for treasure."

"You got an idea?"

"Sure. Rip Heggety can't keep tag on us all the time. Even if he's watching us work, this is still touch-and-go for him, too. I'm going out to track him down. But not just yet. We'll make some noise just so that he'll figure we're keeping to the deal. After a while I'll slip out . . . "

"I'll help you get that rat!" Tommy was anxious to assist his sister and spoke like an impetuous youth.

"You'll stay right here." And that was the way they worked it. They pitched into some work and cleared more rock and rubble from the old mysterious cave, discovering some Indian hieroglyphics and drawings of buffaloes. They made a lot of noise in one way or the other. Then Wade figuring the light was too poor for the concealed Heggety man to see everything, crept out, getting to the nearest cranny. He spent about thirty seconds there and then moved on, carefully, because he did not wish to give the slightest hint to the hidden man, if he was watching, that some trick was about to be played.

Wade knew the dangers, not that he was thinking about himself. He had this constant picture of Stella and the potential danger to her, and it created a vile anger inside him. Just to know she was in this danger sharpened his realisation that he was in love with her. Yeah, it was true, and he was facing the truth. He, the man who had lived hard and never wanted it any other way, felt a surging love for this girl. And God help the man who harmed her!

He was out to get Heggety for good. The man had earned his fate and it could only be death. But even death for Heggety would have to wait until Stella was located.

Wade crept bitterly into another crevice, of which there were plenty, and in this manner got some distance from the Indian cave before he glanced back. He could see the dark shapes of Tommy and Dave as they moved around the site among the deeper shadows. If Heggety was watching the same scene, then it was barely possible for the man to keep an exact check on the men. At the best they were only shapes in the night and mistakes could easily be made.

He crept to a biggish boulder and then sank out of sight, another shape in the gloom. The moon was obscured, giving only limited illumination. He looked around in a concentrated effort to locate Heggety. The man had got to be somewhere in a ring around the cave site. He couldn't be too far away or he'd defeat himself. He was obviously behind some damned boulder or rock. He would not be lying on the flat canyon floor because that didn't provide cover — although anything was possible in this cat-and-mouse game.

Suddenly, remembering an old Indian trick, Wade put his hands to his mouth and made a low howling noise, like a night hyena on the prowl and baying to the moon.

He waited, staring keenly all around, desperate to penetrate the night, urgent to find Stella.

Almost immediately a harsh voice snarled an oath and a stone whizzed though the air.

Wade grinned thinly. So somebody was trying to scare away the banshee hyena!

He blessed the good fortune that had prompted him to think of the old hyena trick. The Indians used this device. It befitted this dark silent canyon with its legends of ancient Indian tribes. But musing about this old place would get him nowhere.

He had noted the spot from where the curse and the stone had come. He let the night fall around him for a little longer and then he began to slide forward on his belly. He moved so quietly he made no more noise than a snake.

After a minute of going in the direction of the curse, he became aware of the man lying flat behind the medium-sized boulder. This man must be Heggety, although he was simply a shape in the night, keeping his cunning watch on the site of the Siomi cave.

The man was lying flat on his stomach, his hat level with the top of the boulder, watching. Heggety certainly had some predatory patience. He seemed to have no suspicion that one of the men from the cave was missing.

The trouble was, Wade knew he could not just shoot the man dead. This was not reluctance about killing. There was the real danger that Stella would never be found and perish somewhere among the chaos of jumbled boulders that stretched for a long way around the base of the canyon walls.

That fate was unthinkable. There had to be another way.

But if Wade could not shoot Heggety in cold blood, that man was not bound by any such considerations towards Wade! If the hellion suspected he was being stalked, out would come his gun.

It was pretty obvious that all Heggety's concentration was centred on the cave-mouth and the dark shapes of the men. Wade was sure he must be making some sound in the night, but seemingly they were unnoticed by the other man.

And then it was possible for Wade to leap forward. He flew through the night air and landed with a tremendous thump on Heggety's back. The man, warned at the last split second, as was inevitable, tried to draw a gun but never got it clear of the leather.

Wade smashed a left and a right into the hateful face. Then, despite this punishment, the man tried to bring his knee up into Wade's guts. Wade rolled and jabbed viciously at Heggety's face again but this did not seem to smash the guy. He was hard as iron.

It was not the time for nice behaviour; too much was at stake. Wade shoved a hand down for his gun, brought it out. He had the advantage in that he was straddling the man, his weight keeping him down. Wade thudded the Colt butt to the side of Heggety's head. This brought a hideous gasp of pain from the man and he seemed to sink.

But within seconds he was full of fight, struggling, hissing and uttering threats. Wade rammed the gun-butt at the man's head again and this really dazed him.

"Get up! Take me to the girl! I'll gun-whip you every time you show fight! In fact, I'll gun-whip you every ten yards if I figure you need it! Now move it. I want to find Stella pronto — before she is bitten by a snake or something."

As Rip Heggety staggered to his feet, swaying under the punishment he had received, Wade plucked his six-shooter from its holster and felt safer. "Get going."

The hell-bent man staggered along, out of his cover, the fight seemingly drained from him.

But such was his bull-like nature he tried to make a break a few moments later. Wade was ready as the man jerked. The gun-butt whipped across again and nearly felled the man. Gasping horribly, Heggety staggered along under Wade's direction.

"Don't try it again, feller!"

But the fight was out of the man. It was impossible for him to take more punishment. He kept on his feet staggering as Wade impelled him forward. They climbed the rocky pile-up and Heggety showed Wade the huge hole where the girl lay gagged and bound.

Wade felled the man without mercy, banking on him being out cold for a long time — time enough to help the girl. With a leap, Wade was beside her. His knife cut the ropes and his fingers gently untied the gag.

"Stella — my — dear — " He couldn't find the right words, not that words really mattered right then. Then she fell into his embrace and he knew everything would be all right for them both.

The gold would be found. Ownership would be proved. And Rip Heggety would meet justice for his crimes.

Wade picked the girl up and carried her to the camp-fire near the cave. Tommy and Dave crowded around. "Stella thank goodness you're safe!" She glanced up at her brother, smiling. Dave Latimer was overjoyed, too.

They built up the fire now that they were safe from hellion attack. Heggety was the mainspring — and he was a captive man. They had brought him to the fire, insensible, and tied him with rope.

The gold was forgotten. In any event, they had not yet located the stuff. But somehow they all felt sure the precious yellow metal was there, as it had been for centuries perhaps.

As for Stella, she was overjoyed at being found. A special kind of happiness glowed in her eyes when she looked at the tall tough man, Wade Tulane.

As for Wade, he realised he would have to clear himself of the wanted charge if he was to have a future. So far he had simply run away. For the first time, he knew he'd been a fool, on this matter at least. He would get the stupid business cleared up — for Stella's sake if nothing else, because where she was he'd want to be in future.

"The end of the trail," he murmured, and lit a cigarette. He glanced at Stella. "You'll find the gold . . . "

"We've deserved it," she smiled.

"Do good by it," said Dave Latimer.

Tommy grinned. "You bet! We've got roots in this town and we want to see it grow into something good. And I've a notion that Wade will be right with us from now on!"

There was a laugh all round.

A day later, as a sort of epilogue, Wade met the sheriff. "Hey, Tulane. I've got a duplicate of a wanted poster on you."

"Yeah?"

Bill Hapner grinned. "Another notice was circulated with it. Seems up there in Cactus Plain there are a lot of men who are ready to swear it was self-defence. You're in the clear."

Wade Tulane nodded and went on his way.

Other titles in the Linford Western Library:

TOP HAND
Wade Everett

The Broken T was big. But no ranch is big enough to let a man hide from himself.

GUN WOLVES OF LOBO BASIN
Lee Floren

The Feud was a blood debt. When Smoke Talbot found the outlaws who gunned down his folks he aimed to nail their hide to the barn door.

SHOTGUN SHARKEY
Marshall Grover

The westbound coach carrying the indomitable Larry and Stretch headed for a shooting showdown.

FIGHTING RAMROD
Charles N. Heckelmann

Most men would have cut their losses, but Frazer counted the bullets in his guns and said he'd soak the range in blood before he'd give up another inch of what was his.

LONE GUN
Eric Allen

Smoke Blackbird had been away too long. The Lequires had seized the Blackbird farm, forcing the Indians and settlers off, and no one seemed willing to fight! He had to fight alone.

THE THIRD RIDER
Barry Cord

Mel Rawlins wasn't going to let anything stand in his way. His father was murdered, his two brothers gone. Now Mel rode for vengeance.

ARIZONA DRIFTERS
W. C. Tuttle

When drifting Dutton and Lonnie Steelman decide to become partners they find that they have a common enemy in the formidable Thurston brothers.

TOMBSTONE
Matt Braun

Wells Fargo paid Luke Starbuck to outgun the silver-thieving stagecoach gang at Tombstone. Before long Luke can see the only thing bearing fruit in this eldorado will be the gallows tree.

HIGH BORDER RIDERS
Lee Floren

Buckshot McKee and Tortilla Joe cut the trail of a border tough who was running Mexican beef into Texas. They stopped the smuggler in his tracks.

BRETT RANDALL, GAMBLER
E. B. Mann

Larry Day had the choice of running away from the law or of assuming a dead man's place. No matter what he decided he was bound to end up dead.

THE GUNSHARP
William R. Cox

The Eggerleys weren't very smart. They trained their sights on Will Carney and Arizona's biggest blood bath began.

THE DEPUTY OF SAN RIANO
Lawrence A. Keating and Al. P. Nelson

When a man fell dead from his horse, Ed Grant was spotted riding away from the scene. The deputy sheriff rode out after him and came up against everything from gunfire to dynamite.

FARGO: MASSACRE RIVER
John Benteen

The ambushers up ahead had now blocked the road. Fargo's convoy was a jumble, a perfect target for the insurgents' weapons!

SUNDANCE: DEATH IN THE LAVA
John Benteen

The Modoc's captured the wagon train and its cargo of gold. But now the halfbreed they called Sundance was going after it . . .

HARSH RECKONING
Phil Ketchum

Five years of keeping himself alive in a brutal prison had made Brand tough and careless about who he gunned down . . .

FARGO: PANAMA GOLD
John Benteen

With foreign money behind him, Buckner was going to destroy the Panama Canal before it could be completed. Fargo's job was to stop Buckner.

FARGO: THE SHARPSHOOTERS
John Benteen

The Canfield clan, thirty strong were raising hell in Texas. Fargo was tough enough to hold his own against the whole clan.

PISTOL LAW
Paul Evan Lehman

Lance Jones came back to Mustang for just one thing — revenge! Revenge on the people who had him thrown in jail.

HELL RIDERS
Steve Mensing

Wade Walker's kid brother, Duane, was locked up in the Silver City jail facing a rope at dawn. Wade was a ruthless outlaw, but he was smart, and he had vowed to have his brother out of jail before morning!

DESERT OF THE DAMNED
Nelson Nye

The law was after him for the murder of a marshal — a murder he didn't commit. Breen was after him for revenge — and Breen wouldn't stop at anything . . . blackmail, a frameup . . . or murder.

DAY OF THE COMANCHEROS
Steven C. Lawrence

Their very name struck terror into men's hearts — the Comancheros, a savage army of cutthroats who swept across Texas, leaving behind a bloodstained trail of robbery and murder.

SUNDANCE: SILENT ENEMY
John Benteen

A lone crazed Cheyenne was on a personal war path. They needed to pit one man against one crazed Indian. That man was Sundance.

LASSITER
Jack Slade

Lassiter wasn't the kind of man to listen to reason. Cross him once and he'll hold a grudge for years to come — if he let you live that long.

LAST STAGE TO GOMORRAH
Barry Cord

Jeff Carter, tough ex-riverboat gambler, now had himself a horse ranch that kept him free from gunfights and card games. Until Sturvesant of Wells Fargo showed up.

McALLISTER ON THE COMANCHE CROSSING
Matt Chisholm

The Comanche, McAllister owes them a life — and the trail is soaked with the blood of the men who had tried to outrun them before.

QUICK-TRIGGER COUNTRY
Clem Colt

Turkey Red hooked up with Curly Bill Graham's outlaw crew. But wholesale murder was out of Turk's line, so when range war flared he bucked the whole border gang alone . . .

CAMPAIGNING
Jim Miller

Ambushed on the Santa Fe trail, Sean Callahan is saved by two Indian strangers. But there'll be more lead and arrows flying before the band join Kit Carson against the Comanches.

GUNSLINGER'S RANGE
Jackson Cole

Three escaped convicts are out for revenge. They won't rest until they put a bullet through the head of the dirty snake who locked them behind bars.

RUSTLER'S TRAIL
Lee Floren

Jim Carlin knew he would have to stand up and fight because he had staked his claim right in the middle of Big Ike Outland's best grass.

THE TRUTH ABOUT SNAKE RIDGE
Marshall Grover

The troubleshooters came to San Cristobal to help the needy. For Larry and Stretch the turmoil began with a brawl and then an ambush.

WOLF DOG RANGE
Lee Floren

Will Ardery would stop at nothing, unless something stopped him first — like a bullet from Pete Manly's gun.

DEVIL'S DINERO
Marshall Grover

Plagued by remorse, a rich old reprobate hired the Texas Trouble-shooters to deliver a fortune in greenbacks to each of his victims.

GUNS OF FURY
Ernest Haycox

Dane Starr, alias Dan Smith, wanted to close the door on his past and hang up his guns, but people wouldn't let him.

DONOVAN
Elmer Kelton

Donovan was supposed to be dead. Uncle Joe Vickers had fired off both barrels of a shotgun into the vicious outlaw's face as he was escaping from jail. Now Uncle Joe had been shot — in just the same way.

CODE OF THE GUN
Gordon D. Shirreffs

MacLean came riding home, with saddle tramp written all over him, but sewn in his shirt-lining was an Arizona Ranger's star.

GAMBLER'S GUN LUCK
Brett Austen

Gamblers seldom live long. Parker was a hell of a gambler. It was his life — or his death . . .